Austin

The Adlers

By
Avery Gale

PUBLISHER
Avery Gale
averygale.com

Cover Design by Jess Buffett at Sinfully Sweet Designs
Editing by Sandy Ebel at Personal Touch Editing
Proofreading and Second Edits by Karen Bailey

The Adlers

The siblings. Their occupations and ages at the beginning of the series:

Austin – 31 – CEO of the family oil conglomerate based in Austin, TX.

Asia – 30 – Ruthless legal eagle for the family business.

Bronx – 29 – Owns a string of car dealerships in partnership with brother, Cleveland.

Cleveland – 28 – Race car driver.

Brooklyn – 27 – Retrieval expert for big insurance companies. Semi-retired in subsequent books. Security consultant. Married to Luke Grayson, lives in New Mexico.

Catalina – 26 – Freelance intelligent agent, working with the CIA, MI6, Mossad, and others. Travels the world as a successful jewelry designer.

Israel – 25– Security expert and tracker.

Kensington – 24 – Actor.

London – 23 – Chemist/Researcher. Married to shifters, Elijah & Evan Monroe, lives outside Boston.

Paris – 22 – College student.

Watch this page for updates in subsequent books in this series.

A note to readers...

All the books in The Adlers series will focus on one of the ten Adler siblings, but they will also include numerous side stories intended to keep you connected to the family and lay groundwork for future installments.

Those asides are not random, they are intentional.

Thank you for letting me share my passion with you...your friendship and support mean so much more than you know.

A ery Gale

Chapter One

AUSTIN ADLER STOOD in the shadows watching as his brother, Israel, flogged one of the unattached submissives at the Prairie Winds Club. The petite brunette's lightly tanned skin practically glowed with the deep pink lash marks Israel loved so much. Initially, the wide strips of the supple deer hide flogger would feel little more than a warm caress of her skin. The impact implement provided a deceptive warm-up before Israel altered the angle and intensity in small increments. By the time he intensified the blows, the pretty little sub would already be too close to an endorphin-induced state of bliss to care. He and Israel maintained memberships to several kink clubs around the world, but Prairie Winds outside Austin, Texas and Dark Desires in downtown Houston were the two Austin favored.

Israel Adler had always been as sexually dominant as Austin, but the brothers' tastes were vastly different in subtle ways. Israel played hard and provided tender aftercare that turned the most jaded subs into his most loyal admirers, then walked away without looking back. The younger Adler was always upfront with the subs he played with during their initial scene negotiations. Israel pulled no punches—never led them to believe their relationship would ever be anything more than what they'd agreed on—because it wouldn't.

Rarely playing with the same submissive more than a few times, Israel repeatedly said he had no plans to look for a long-term relationship anytime soon. There were times Austin envied his younger brother's carefree lifestyle. Israel's skill with a flogger and his ability to remain friendly with the subs he walked away from made him one of the most sought out Doms in several clubs around the country. Austin often wondered how Israel was going to react when the Universe finally set the younger man's mate on his path.

Lifting his gaze from the small stage, Austin scanned the room, his attention drawn to a slender figure standing at the outer edge of the room shrouded in shadow. She was standing as close as possible to one of the moveable partitions the club used to reshape the large main room into smaller, more intimate spaces, her attention captured by the scene. Even though she was partially shadowed, there was something hauntingly familiar about her. Even without a clear view, Austin knew the petite subbie was transfixed, the intensity of the scene touching her soul as deep-seated need pulsed within her.

The unmistakable aroma of sex had surrounded Austin since he'd walked through the club's front door, but now, the musky tendrils tickling his nose carried a different scent—one that called to his wolf on such an elemental level, it was impossible to ignore. Inhaling deeply, he felt his nostrils flare, the unique aroma imprinting itself on his soul. *Mine!* Trying to shake off the unappreciated wave of possessiveness washing over him, Austin narrowed his eyes, trying to identify the woman whose soul seemed to be reaching out to touch his.

"Do you know her?" Austin turned his gaze to the man who'd stepped up beside him and shrugged. A year ago, Austin would have been surprised to see the owner of Dark Desires, Cameron Barnes, at Prairie Winds, but after Cam and his growing family moved less than five minutes down the road, he and his wife had become club regulars. Turning back, he felt the woman across the room studying him, her eyes widening in recognition a split second before she vanished in a silvery mist.

"What the fuck? Did she just disappear into thin air?" Austin had known Cam for years and could honestly say this was the first time he'd seen the former CIA agent flustered. "What the hell? Do you know her?"

Austin hadn't answered the first time because he'd wanted to get a better look—now the elusive woman had made certain he wouldn't be able to confirm her identity. It took him several seconds to find his voice—he didn't know what surprised him more, finding her in a kink club or the shocking realization she'd just shimmered out of sight. Fucking shimmered! He'd read about the magical ability in the ancient tomes, but he'd never known anyone who could do it. Hell, he'd never even talked to anyone who had seen it.

"Yes, or at least I believe so. I could have sworn the woman was my assistant, but I had no idea she was into kink." In his peripheral vision, Austin saw Cam staring at him, his mouth gaping open in disbelief.

"She fucking disappears into a shiny mist, and you're

astonished she's into kink? Are you fucking kidding me? Holy hell. I want to meet her—arrange it. The implications of this are so far reaching, I don't even know where to begin."

Despite their years-long friendship, Austin couldn't remember Cam ever asking him for a favor, so there wasn't a chance in hell he would deny the man an introduction, but he wanted answers from Ms. Charlotte Hays first—and he wanted them now.

"Excuse me. I'm going to find my vanishing right-hand." Cam was still muttering in disbelief as Austin stomped around the perimeter, trying to make his way to where he'd last seen Charlotte when he'd felt her eyes lock on his. How the hell had he missed the fact she was a magical? And more importantly, how had the little minx managed to hide her submissive side—because there was no doubt in his mind, the woman standing across the room was a sub—hell, desire had been coming off her in waves until she'd seen him watching her.

He would do his best to track her down tonight, but if she managed to elude him, she wouldn't be able to avoid him for long. Austin knew precisely when he'd have another opportunity because he knew precisely what time his admin would enter the Adler Oil inner sanctum Monday morning.

You cannot hide forever, Charlotte.

SHIT. SHIT. SHIT. I thought he said he was leaving town for the weekend. Fuckity fuck. Charlotte Hays had been so engrossed in Israel Adler's scene, she hadn't noticed Austin standing across the room until it was too late. Damn it to goose feathers and duckbills.

When she'd first arrived, Charlotte had asked if Austin was inside, but the man everyone called Tank had shaken his head and given her a stern reminder about the club's strict confidentiality agreement she'd signed when she first joined several months earlier. During her extensive research, prior to joining the club, she'd learned the contract they called an agreement was one of the strictest in the kink world, and several of their associate clubs used the same document. Breaching it spelled disaster on several levels. Careers crashed overnight, and the loose-lipped offender found themselves facing legal and personal challenges that drained resources and cut them off from everyone associated with the network's clubs. In other words, life as you knew it vanished into thin air, much as she'd just done... in a room full of people. *Fucking dandy.*

She wasn't a fool, screwing up her membership to Prairie Winds wasn't a thought she wanted to entertain. Charlotte appreciated the fact her membership at Prairie Winds would allow her to visit any of the other clubs in the network and offered a reduced membership rate if she should decide to join one of the other establishments. Of course, the only other club close enough for her to attend was Dark Desires in Houston, and after the damned disappearing act she'd just pulled in front of the club owner, Cameron Barnes, that option was probably off the table now.

Moving swiftly along the outer wall of the main room, Charlotte was careful to avoid bumping into anyone.

Taking a deep breath to steady her nerves, she knew she needed to slow down. Several people had felt the cool brush of air as she passed and turned to see who'd moved up alongside them. Their surprise to find nothing but empty space was blatantly obvious. If Austin was looking for her, their reactions would give her away in a New York minute.

Charlotte had researched Austin for two years—studying his habits, likes, and particularly, the things he disliked. Discovering he was a sexual dominant had been a bonus in her opinion since it was something she'd been reading about since she got her first e-reader. She'd filled the device with so many steamy novels, it was a wonder it hadn't spontaneously combusted.

Looking behind her, Charlotte saw Austin was indeed searching for her and gaining fast, from the looks of it. Turning back around, she was startled to see Tobi West standing close... much too close. Bumping into the petite blonde hard enough to knock her off balance, Charlotte was forced to reach for the other woman to keep her from tumbling to the floor. The effort required to keep the vivacious wife of club owners, Kent and Kyle West, from tumbling to the floor divided Charlotte's focus. Damn it all to hell, maintaining a shimmer disappearance required a tremendous amount of concentration. Her frantic effort to help Tobi stay on her feet was too distracting, and despite Charlotte's haste to escape, she knew it was all simply too much.

"Holy shit-sus, Charlotte, I didn't see you coming." Tobi's voice held a note of uncertainty because she'd been looking forward and would have certainly seen Charlotte...

if she'd been visible.

"Nobody saw her coming, Tobi." Austin wrapped his large hand around her upper arm as he steadied Tobi with the other. "Are you okay, or would you like me to find one of your husbands?" Austin's even tone didn't fool Charlotte, she heard the thread of steel laced through his question and hoped upon hope her muddled mind could come up with a plausible explanation before it was too late.

"I'm right here, Austin. Thank you both for keeping my lovely wife from dropping to the floor." Kyle West stepped forward, wrapping his arms around Tobi, pressing a kiss to the top of her head. "I can't let you out of my sight for a minute, Kitten, you are a trouble magnet."

"I can assure you, this time wasn't your sweet sub's fault." Austin hadn't released Charlotte's arm, his grip firm, but not so much he risked bruising her. When he felt her tense, preparing to step away, his fingers flexed subtly, letting her know she wasn't going anywhere.

"As I said, she is a magnet for mischief, it just finds her. It's amazing really." Shifting his attention from Tobi to Charlotte, Kyle tilted his head to the side as he studied her. "I was standing across the room, not far from Austin a few minutes ago." *Oh shit.* She was so screwed. "I'm looking forward to hearing an explanation for what I saw but believe Austin has called first dibs. I'll wait, but not long, so don't be a stranger, Charlotte."

"I'll set up something after London's wedding." Austin had already planned for Charlotte to attend so they could work between the scheduled events. Looking down at her, his dark eyes shining with focused intent, Austin continued, "Cam wants to talk to her as well."

To anyone who didn't know him well, Austin's tone would have sounded impassive, but she wasn't fooled. Austin Adler wasn't going to be happy until he was convinced he'd uncovered every one of her secrets. She was going to have to think fast to keep from blowing her objective. She didn't have everything in place yet, it was too early to reveal her purpose. Until she knew what he had planned for her home, she wouldn't know how to counter it.

Damn it all to hell, a few more months and she'd have everything lined out. She should have double checked to make certain Austin had actually left town as he'd planned to. Had Charlotte known Israel was in town before walking up to find him flogging a sub into orbit, she might have anticipated Austin's change in plans, but since she didn't have access to the younger Adler's calendar, she hadn't realized he was home.

Standing beside Austin, she felt another presence. Turning, she saw Israel leaning casually against the wall beside her. Shaking his head, a wicked grin tilting the corners of his mouth, he sent her a knowing look.

"What did you do, Miss Charlotte? Big brother looks like he's about ready to blow a gasket." He'd barely spoken the words, but she'd heard not only the question but the amusement in his tone.

Dandy, just what I need, two shifters interrogating me... and to add gas to the flame, let's make sure one of them is my boss and the other a damned tracker who can spot deception at a thousand paces. Israel Adler was unnaturally good at his job, making her wonder what sort of gifts he possessed... aside from being a shifter. Neither of them knew *she knew*, nor did they know she'd watched them shift and run into the wooded area running along the Colorado River and around Lake Travis.

The first time she'd watched them, Charlotte had been so transfixed, she'd dropped her shimmer when they stripped out of their clothes. Their ripped bodies were pure perfection—she'd suddenly understood why people write poetry and song lyrics about such moments. Thank the gods she'd been well hidden, the last thing she'd needed was for them to spot her. She'd also sent up a silent prayer of thanks she'd had the foresight to make certain she'd been downwind, so they didn't scent her—the warm rush of moisture soaking her panties at the sight of their long cocks swelling as their bodies shifted would have given her away instantly. Hearing the two brothers often shared their lovers had piqued Charlotte's interest, but she didn't know whether or not it was true since she'd made a concerted effort to avoid the club when she suspected they might be in attendance.

Hearing a growl from Austin, Charlotte looked up at the man still holding her arm and blinked in confusion. Had he asked her a question? Oh hell, she'd been busy thinking about how amazing he and Israel looked naked and hadn't been paying attention. Deciding to apologize and try to slip her arm from his hold, Charlotte turned to Tobi and smiled.

"I'm really sorry I bulldozed you. I was looking behind me instead of where I was going. You'd think I'd learn, but it seems I'm doomed to a life of being a klutz." Trying to gently wiggle her arm free as she'd spoken hadn't worked, the damned man kept his enormous paw securely wrapped around her bicep. *Pun intended.* A snort of laughter from Israel made her gasp. Was he able to hear her thoughts? As unlikely as it seemed, she knew Brooklyn Adler's fiancé was a gifted empath, so it wasn't impossible.

Israel stepped closer, grasping her other arm, mirroring Austin's hold. She was convinced the two men were communicating telepathically, but there was no way to be sure. Israel flashed her a smile that told her he was either listening to her thoughts or too damned observant for his own good… and neither option boded well for her.

"Let's go. We need to have a long talk." *We? Need? Nope.* Leaning down, his warm breath caressing the shell of her ear, Austin added, "I'd blank my mind for a bit if I were you—no reason to give my brother any more ammunition."

So, he does read minds. Just fucking dandy.

Chapter Two

ISRAEL FELT THE energy in the room shift as he brought the pretty dark-haired club submissive back to earth after sending her into subspace. The endorphin induced state usually eluded this particular sub, so he'd been thrilled to see her body respond so perfectly. Deputy Berlin Fox was not only a beautiful woman, she was also incredibly intelligent—the fact her kinks matched his was a bonus. If he were ever looking for a long-term relationship, Berlin would be the first woman he sought out. Oddly enough, they'd become friends outside the club, thanks to crossing paths professionally on a couple of cases.

Proving she was not only bright but intuitive as well, she looked up at him from the over-stuffed leather sofa where he settled her while he'd cleaned the equipment and shook her head as he approached.

"No, I don't need anything, Sir. Go find out what the hell all the ruckus is about." When he raised his brows in surprise, her husky laugh cut through the guilt he'd been feeling about walking away before providing the level of aftercare the subs he played with had come to expect. "Guilt is overrated, Sir. Go." Her eyes were still soft from the endorphin high the flogging had given her, making her look flushed and well-sated—his favorite look on a submissive.

Leaning down, he threaded his fingers through her chestnut locks, fisting her hair tight enough to tip her face up to meet his gaze. Sealing his lips over hers in a searing kiss, guaranteed to fuel his fantasies until he returned to Prairie Winds, he took everything she was willing to give before pulling back.

"You were magnificent, pet. I'm looking forward to playing with you again. I am leaving the country for a family wedding, but I want you to know how honored I am you have entrusted yourself to me. You're beautiful and brilliant, and I'm looking forward to rewarding your generous heart, Berlin." Her face softened for a split second before he saw her suck in a deep breath. *And there it is—the look of a woman reminding herself about everything she's heard about my reputation.*

"Drive carefully if I don't see you before you leave." She nodded before darting her eyes to the side of the room where people seemed to be gathering around his brother and Kyle West. *Time to go.*

Sending his bag to the locker room with one of the club's male subs, he smiled when the young bodybuilder hefted the bag without effort. Giving the scantily clothed man a nod of thanks, Israel moved to where his brother stood holding his administrative assistant by the upper arm. From the look on Austin's face, he was battling to remain in control—the look of barely restrained frustration wasn't the norm for the head of Adler Oil. Since their parents' death, Austin had been the picture of single-minded focus, rebuilding their crumbling inheritance into a corporate powerhouse—not an easy feat and not one accomplished by overreacting emotionally. *Interesting.*

Staying to the side, Israel listened to the tense conversation playing out in front of him. Unsure what the petite, auburn-haired beauty—who ordinarily tried to be virtually invisible—had done to rile up her boss, Israel decide to tune in to her instead. Part of what made him a world-renowned tracker was his ability to listen to his target's internal dialogue—often he could see what the other person was seeing as well—but Charlotte's mind was spinning so fast, he was only catching disjointed bits and pieces. The pictures popping like damned balloons in her mind seemed to sparkle. *What the hell is with all the fucking glitter?*

He had more questions than answers at this point, but the one thing Israel knew for sure was that Miss Charlotte had just landed dead center on Austin's kink radar. Of all the questions he was hearing from his older brother, one kept surging to the forefront. Big brother wanted the woman he was holding so firmly, she was literally dancing on tip-toes.

AUSTIN TURNED TOWARD the locker rooms, wanting to put some distance between them and the Wests before speaking. Once they were out of earshot, he rounded on his wayward admin.

"You and I will wait in the hall while Israel gathers his things, then we'll ask the women's room attendant to retrieve yours." When she opened her mouth to speak, he held up his free hand. "Don't argue with me, Charlotte. I am not in the fucking mood." When she attempted to put the brakes on, he and Israel simply lifted her off her feet. To anyone not paying close attention, it would appear she was keeping pace with their gigantic steps, which was a fucking irony in itself since she was no match for their size.

"Charlotte, I'm looking forward to hearing about your moonlit trip to the lake." Israel might have sounded as though he was making casual conversation, but Austin knew better. *I'm not getting it all, but I've gotten enough to figure it out. She knows we're shifters, she's watched—more than once.* Israel's words moved easily in Austin's mind, and he felt his lips firm into a grim line. Wondering once again how he'd managed to miss she was a magical, Austin watched his brother disappear into the locker room. When his petite prisoner opened her mouth to speak, he shook his head.

"Don't say a word. Not one." She glowered at him, and he gave her a feral grin. "You will be given an opportunity to explain—as a matter of fact, I'm looking forward to it— but for now, I'm not letting you out of my sight."

"I was only going to let you know there is no reason to stop at the locker room. My coat is checked in at the front desk." Her pout was adorable, and for the first time since he'd finally gotten his hands on her, Austin was able to dial back his annoyance a bit.

"Thank you, I appreciate the clarification. Where is your car parked?" He felt her stiffen beneath his hold as her eyes went wide with something that looked a lot like embarrassment. *What the hell was that about?* "Don't even think about lying to me. I *will* know, and you are already in deep enough." Her shoulders stiffened for a few seconds before slumping.

"It's at the back of the lot, and before you lecture me about parking so far from the building, I'd like to remind you I'm not without resources to avoid a dangerous situation." *Of course, you'd never know it by the cluster fuck I've created tonight, but I'm usually damned good at flying under everyone's radar.*

Israel emerged a few minutes later, freshly showered, carrying his toy bag. Austin led them to the front. After helping her into her coat, Austin held out the small suitcase the coat check attendant called a purse.

"Her car is parked at the far end of the lot." Israel frowned at her before returning his attention to Austin. "I'll drive you down to it, so you have the lights. Miss Shimmer out of fucking sight will be riding with me." *Penthouse.* Since he'd sent a text to the valet, his truck was already waiting when they stepped outside.

Charlotte's thin jacket was no match for the chilly evening air, so Austin stopped long enough to wrap his own coat around her, smiling to himself when it engulfed her. Moving quickly down the stone steps, he gave the young valet a generous tip, knowing the young man was working two different jobs as he finished his graduate studies in finance. Austin had encouraged him to apply at Adler Oil when he graduated next year and was certain several other club members had probably extended similar offers. Driving to the dark corner of the lot, Austin couldn't believe his eyes.

"Is *that* your car? You drove *that mechanical disaster* all the way out here? At night? *Alone?*" He was literally starting to see red tinges at the edge of his vision as the full implication slammed into him.

"I'll admit, it's not much to look at, but it runs okay... most of the time... usually."

He heard Israel's snort of laughter and shook his head. Their sisters had driven the Adler men to distraction with their lack of interest in the safety of the automobiles they drove. His brother, Bronx, who now owned numerous auto dealerships in partnership with brother Cleveland, made certain his sisters owned mechanically sound vehicles. Asia was the only one who'd finally taken an interest in what she drove, regularly updating her sporty choices, thanks to her brothers' guidance—and hefty family discount.

"Charlotte, you make good money. You could buy a decent car." He knew she lived in a small apartment too far from the office to walk, which meant she'd been driving that piece of shit to and from the office, yet he hadn't seen it in the parking garage—it wasn't something he'd miss. "Where do you park when you drive to work?" Charlotte's negligent shrug was too deliberate and set off all his internal alarms.

"Here and there. Wherever I can find a space." *Yeah, like down the fucking block.*

She needed to remember he had five—FIVE—younger sisters. If she wanted to blow smoke up his ass, she needed to up her game. He knew she wasn't parking in any of the spaces allotted to Adler employees—there wasn't a chance in hell he'd have missed the death trap illuminated in his headlights.

"Give me your keys, Charlotte." Israel waited, hand

extended while she dug through her cavernous purse. Austin saw his brother sigh and shake his head. "I've never understood why women want to carry everything they own with them. Hell, the weight alone is an issue." Even in the dark, Austin saw Charlotte roll her eyes.

"This is your only warning, sweetness. Rolling your eyes at a Dom is not smart, and you've already dug yourself in mighty deep." There was a part of him that wished she would roll her eyes again. Paddling her ass would be therapeutic—for both of them. He didn't doubt for a moment she was going to minimize what happened inside the club. She might be his personal administrative assistant, but they hadn't worked together long enough for her to have a clear view of how resolute he could be.

Resolute, my ass. You're the most stubborn bastard on the planet. Israel's teasing voice moved through his mind, the connection distracting him enough to take a deep breath. *If she ever finds her keys, I'll follow you.* Austin watched in amazement as she seemed to pull everything but her keys from what looked more like a piece of carry-on luggage than a purse.

"It's nice to do this sitting down... where it's warm."

Austin felt his grip tighten on the steering wheel as a vision of her standing alongside her damned car, her attention focused on inside her bag rather than on her surroundings caused him to see red. *She needs a fucking keeper.*

"Charlotte, if I ever catch you standing alongside your car, looking for your keys, I'll paddle your bare ass until you can't sit down for a week. Do you know the danger you put yourself in by not being attentive to your surroundings?" He groaned when she held up the keys in triumph. Hell, she hadn't heard a word he'd said. Dropping the keys in Israel's hand, she grimaced.

"You'll have to hold the clutch in just the right spot for it to start, and it might take a time or two for the motor to stay running." Anything else she would have added was a waste of effort since Israel was already closing the door.

I'll call Bronx and make sure she has something by morning. Hell, I'm tempted to leave the damned keys in it and park it on the fucking street in hopes some fool steals it. Austin fought to keep from smiling as Israel's comment moved through his mind. The two of them often thought along the same line, it was one of the reasons they worked well together sharing subs.

The drive to Adler Oil didn't ordinarily seem long, but tonight it was interminable. Austin let Charlotte sit silently in the passenger seat she'd scrambled into as soon as Israel vacated it. She fastened her seat belt before he could move to help her—a habit he would break in short order—then turned to stare out into the inky darkness. Damn, the woman was so still, he wondered more than once if she was even breathing. Breathing in her scent was as enlightening as it was frustrating. Charlotte Hays was a puzzle, and the number and complexity of the questions tumbling through his mind were growing by leaps and bounds.

After parking his truck, Austin placed his warm palm on her forearm and shook his head when the little magical pixie started to open her own door.

"I can open my own door, Austin."

"I'm sure you can." Some things simply were not open to discussion, and common courtesy was one of them.

"Before we go upstairs, I want to make certain we're on the same page about my expectations. Nothing that has happened tonight will affect our job with Adler Oil. Unless your purpose for being at the club was corporate sabotage, you don't need to worry about career implications." When her gaze dropped and darted to the left, Austin growled. The move told him she planned to lie about what he'd seen at the club.

"How long have you been interested in Dominance and submission?" Austin wasn't prone to wasting time with pleasantries. If he wanted to know something, he asked.

"Several years, but I've only been going to Prairie Winds for a couple of months. I... I haven't been brave enough yet to do anything more than watch."

He nodded to let her know he understood. Austin was more pleased than he should be by her admission. Had he known she was interested in the lifestyle, this discussion would have taken place earlier—*a lot earlier.*

Since hiring her a few weeks ago, Austin continued to find himself drawn to her despite his best efforts to push it to the back of his mind. Somewhere between the club and Adler Oil, his focus seemed to have shifted from interrogating Charlotte about her magical abilities to exploring her kink.

"Tonight is about discovery, Charlotte. If you want to learn about the lifestyle, I'll be the one to teach you." He'd enlist his brother's help—but he'd be the one calling the shots. The thought of someone else introducing her to the joys of sexual fulfillment made him see red at the edges of his vision—again. He'd never been possessive with the women he'd played with, but he was starting to realize none of the old rules applied to Charlotte.

"I will lead, Israel will be our third. He serves at my pleasure."

"I don't know what that means." Her interruption rankled his dominant nature, but he curbed the urge to flip her over his knee—she might understand the basic concept of protocol, but if she hadn't played, the details wouldn't be refined in her mind.

"It means while I may ask you how you feel about having him present, in the end, extending the invitation falls to me." Her lips formed a silent oh, indicating she understood, so he moved on. "Now, don't interrupt again. For tonight, we won't be following high protocol, but that doesn't mean we'll ignore common courtesy." Even in the dim light of the parking garage, Austin saw her cheeks flush with embarrassment.

"Tonight, Israel and I will ask a lot of questions, and we expect you to be completely honest in your responses. Don't sell yourself or your needs short by denying what your soul is searching for." He watched her pupils dilate as her respiration kicked up. Good to know he wasn't the only one affected by their close proximity and the prospect of playing. Her eyes darted back and forth as if searching for a way to hide. *Not happening, sugar.* "Eyes on me, Charlotte." Her eyes locked on his, and Austin could have sworn he felt electricity arc between them.

"I'm a demanding Dom, but I'm fair. I want this to be everything you've hoped for—by Sunday evening, I hope you'll be exhausted, but sated. I promise you'll have a better idea of what the lifestyle can offer you." If he didn't get her into the private elevator that only serviced his and

Asia's respective apartments, he was going to end up fucking her in his damned truck like a hormonal teenager.

"We'll use the club's stoplight system for safe words. Tell me what the words mean to you." He smiled as Charlotte gave him a nearly perfect verbatim recitation of the information found on every club contract he'd ever signed.

"Perfect. As soon as you enter my penthouse, I want you to strip. Lay your dress over the back of the sofa and fold anything else you're wearing, placing it atop your dress. Stand with your back to the fireplace, feet more than shoulder width apart, hands behind your head with your fingers laced together. I want those bright green eyes on me unless otherwise instructed. Do you have any questions about the instructions I've given you?"

Austin watched as she seemed to consider everything he'd said. He appreciated that she hadn't jumped in to give him the answer she thought he wanted. After several seconds, she shook her head.

"Not good enough, Charlotte. Use words. Always."

"No, I don't have any questions about your instructions. That doesn't mean I'm thrilled with the prospect of being naked in front of my boss and his brother, but it seems inevitable if you're going to teach me how to be a submissive."

Giving a curt nod to Israel who'd stepped up beside the passenger door, he watched as his brother helped her down from the four-wheel drive. Once they were inside the elevator, Austin was surprised to see her spine straighten, her shoulders move back, and her gaze locking on him.

"Just so we're clear. I'm not expecting anything past

tonight. I don't know when I'd have finally found the courage to participate in a scene, but I doubt the Wests would have allowed me to continue making excuses. All the signs pointed to them watching me a little too closely." She was probably right. Neither Kent nor Kyle would have waited forever. They were far too experienced to miss a submissive who wasn't getting what he or she needed from the club.

You going to let her go after tonight, bro? Israel's teasing question moved through his mind as they approached the penthouse. *Bastard.* He knew Austin had no intention of limiting their time together. Damned little brothers were obviously still a pain in his ass.

Chapter Three

C HARLOTTE WAS MORE nervous than she'd been during her first visit to Prairie Winds, and she'd almost passed out in the parking lot that night from fear alone. Reminding herself to breathe as the elevator doors slid open, she looked into an entry larger than her entire apartment. Despite her silent demand, willing her feet to move, they seemed rooted in place. Austin's palm pressed against the sensitive spot just above the curve of her ass, the warmth of his touch just enough to thaw her frozen muscles.

Three steps. Looking down, Charlotte's mind whirled with anticipation and fear as she calculated the distance. Just three small steps and she'd cross from the elevator into Austin's penthouse... the space where he expected her to strip off what little clothing she wore and present herself to him. Naked. Exposed. Vulnerable. Reminding herself this was what she'd wanted when she joined the club, Charlotte pulled in a deep breath and took the last steps over the threshold.

"Brave girl."

Israel's compliment warmed the chill she felt stepping onto the pristine marble floor of the penthouse. The stark white floors, white walls, steel and glass furniture all worked together to create a room straight out of Architectural Digest. Looking around, Charlotte suppressed the shudder threatening to surface. Austin's palm pressed firmly against her back, urging her deeper into his personal space. Standing behind the sofa where she was supposed to place her clothing, Charlotte tried to slow her breathing before she hyperventilated.

The black dots dancing in her vision were joined by tiny sparkles she recognized as the beginnings of a shimmer disappearance. Damn it all to dashing donuts, she hadn't spontaneously shimmered due to stress for years.

"Breathe, Charlotte." Austin's low growling command pulled her back to the present. "Eyes on me, sugar." Lifting her gaze to his, she let out a sigh of relief when she didn't see any anger or recrimination in his expression. "Better. Now, give me a color."

"Green. I'm green, Sir." The title slid easily off her tongue since she often referred to him as Sir or Mr. Adler at work. Of course, it would never sound quite the same again in that setting, but she shoved that thought to the back of her mind. *Shimmering would not be in your best interest, Charlotte. Keep your head in the game.* The pep-talk she gave herself was enough to focus her attention on stripping out of her clothing. Toeing off her shoes, Charlotte set them next to the sofa where she'd left her dress before making her way to the fireplace. The room was chilly, and she was grateful when Israel stepped around her to start the gas fireplace. Warmth blanketed her back, and she sighed at the comforting feeling.

Both men watched as she carefully got into the position Austin described while they were still in his truck. She waited for what seemed like an eternity for one of them to speak, the silence killing her. Setting her jaw, she was determined she wouldn't fail this test, and there was no doubt in her mind this was the first of many she'd have to endure.

Austin continued to study her while Israel made subtle adjustments to her position. His touch was anything but clinical, yet it lacked the gentleness and warmth of emotion she would expect from a lover. Frowning at the realization of how easily she would be set aside, Charlotte fought the urge to grab her clothes and run.

"What was that thought?" The biting tone in Austin's voice caused her to jump, breaking position. Israel gave her bare ass a stinging swat before helping her back into the pose he'd so painstakingly perfected seconds earlier. Austin stepped in front of her and using his fingers on her chin, forced her to focus on his face.

"Tell me what you were thinking. Do not lie, Charlotte. I will know."

"I don't lie. If I don't want to tell someone something, I say so." She heard Israel's snort of laughter behind her. Austin didn't appear amused. His fingers firmed on her chin, letting her know he wasn't going to be distracted by her snark.

"I was thinking about Israel's touch. It wasn't completely impersonal, but it wasn't affectionate either. I know you've only agreed to teach me about the lifestyle, but it's kind of depressing to think about how easily you'll move on after... well, after you've taught me about Dominance and submission. I'll be forever changed, but you'll simply shift your attention to the next challenge." Something flickered in Austin's dark eyes, a spark of heat that looked a lot like possessiveness, but it was gone so quickly, she wondered if she'd imagined it.

"Thank you for being so transparent. Your trust humbles me."

She didn't hear any deception or condescension in his tone. She hadn't worked at Adler Oil long, but the one thing she'd learned was Austin Adler was honest to a fault. His comments melted some of the fear of judgment.

"We will demand your honesty, and we'll be equally transparent with you. We'll always answer your questions truthfully. We won't take more than we're willing to give."

Taking a step back, Austin continued his perusal, his gaze like a physical caress. Charlotte felt the heat of the fireplace blanketing her back, but it was the intensity of Austin's regard that was searing the front of her naked body. *Naked... Oh, my heavenly stars and garters! I'm naked in front of Austin and Israel Adler. What the hell was I thinking?*

"She's tipping over the edge, brother." Israel's gravelly voice sounded from her left, but Charlotte didn't turn to look at him. Staying in place was taking all her focus, her fight or flight instinct listing precariously close to flight.

"If she is already close to running, she isn't the woman I thought she was." Austin's barely disguised growl pulled her back from the edge of panic. Using the pad of his finger, he traced an invisible line from her chin down the sensitive column of her neck before pausing at the hollow of her throat. "Any woman as beautiful as this one should never feel insecure. Ivory skin that feels like warm satin and womanly curves begging for my touch combined with the scent of her arousal—she is testing my resolve."

"If you think the front is amazing, brother, wait until you take in the view from the back." Israel paused for a few seconds before whistling softly. "Ms. Charlotte has a world-class ass, and those dimples at the top are enough to make a grown man beg for mercy."

This time Israel's touch was more intimate as his palm swept up the curve of her ass cheeks before settling over the dimples he'd described. The heat from his hand shot directly to her core, sending a flood of moisture to her sex. Sending up a silent prayer, Charlotte hoped they wouldn't notice the flush she could feel moving from her chest up to her face. She heard Israel chuckle behind her.

"I'll save you the trouble of those futile prayers, Sweet Cheeks." Israel emphasized his last words with a quick squeeze to her right cheek. "We'd be able to scent your sweet cream for miles if the wind was in our favor."

AUSTIN STRUGGLED TO hold back the raging desire to sandwich Charlotte between them and claim her as his own. The musky scent of her arousal wrapped itself around him in a stranglehold, threatening to cut off the supply of oxygen to his brain. Hell, who was he kidding, if he were wearing his usual suit pants instead of leathers, his cock would be imitating the world's sturdiest tent pole. Letting his gaze move over her in a slow perusal, Austin was enraptured. Damn, the woman's body was a work of art.

He was grateful his brother picked up the slack when he hadn't been able to push words past the lump in his throat. Desire and apprehension were coming off Charlotte in waves, and the mix was intoxicating.

"Call the esthetician from the spa and set up something here for tomorrow morning." Austin's growled words caused Charlotte to gasp. "I'll forward specifics and instructions while Charlotte is soaking in the tub." He saw tears fill her eyes and stepped closer. "What's wrong?" He watched her open her mouth to speak, but no words came out as tears trailed down her cheeks. Israel stepped around her, frowning when he saw she was crying.

She's blocking me. How the fuck did she learn to do that so quickly? Austin could hear the irritation in his brother's voice.

Don't forget, she's a magical, and we don't know yet what all that entails. I want to know what triggered this response. All I said was I'd send the instructions while she soaked in the tub. Hell, I thought a long, hot bath was every woman's dream.

"I took a shower before I went to the club. I know shifters have a keen sense of smell, but I don't think I could be offensive enough to require a bath and spa treatment." Charlotte's words shocked Austin. Her shaky response sliced his heart, the wounded tone in her voice a punch to the gut. How had he managed to hurt her when he'd merely been trying to treat her like a princess?

"Stop." The sharp tone of his own voice startling her. "The bath was meant as a way to help you relax between this inspection and our time in the playroom, which I expect will push your boundaries further than you think possible. Bringing the esthetician here was meant as a treat. I didn't want you to leave the safety and comfort of my home for the massage and waxing." He hoped she would be open to laser treatments in the future. Keeping her pussy bared to his touch would be a priority.

"I've never had a massage."

Without his enhanced hearing, he'd have missed her whispered admission. He wasn't surprised. One thing he'd learned about his assistant was she was frugal with her money. She rarely joined her co-workers for lunch at their favorite bistros, preferring the sandwiches she brought from home, and after seeing the car she drove, he wondered where the hell her money was going.

"Then you'll enjoy it even more. There is nothing like a long massage to drain away deep-muscle tension. Waxing will bare those pretty pussy lips to our touch. You'll be much more sensitive, and when you kneel with your knees spread, I'll be able to enjoy the view without it being impeded by those lovely auburn curls. As appealing as they are, they hide your delectable mysteries, and there is no room for secrets in a D/s relationship."

"Relationship? I thought you only wanted to teach me about submission tonight. Or maybe for part of the weekend?"

Charlotte was a lot of things, but she wasn't good at hiding her emotions. Even without Israel's empathetic connection, Austin heard the surprise and hope in her voice. She wanted more than the weekend, but for some reason didn't feel she deserved it.

"I don't bring subs I simply plan to play with for a few hours into my home, Charlotte. You are the first woman, other than family, who has been here." He saw her eyes widen in surprise, but she didn't ask any of the questions he knew were swirling around in her sharp mind. It was time to get back on track. He wanted to move her mindset back to the reason she was standing naked in his living room.

"Since you know we are shifters, I assume you also know we are highly sexualized. Plainly stated, that means we like to fuck—often. Israel and I plan to use your sweet body this weekend. You'll be given time to rest, but you will be using muscles you didn't know you had. The massage will help, but I'm a possessive bastard, so I want to manage the contact. No one touches what's mine without my permission and supervision." Her mouth opened in a silent *oh*, but her eyes dilated with arousal. *I think our sweet subbie may be a bit of an exhibitionist.*

Well, won't that be fun to explore? Damn, I love natural submissives who are new to the lifestyle. Israel was all about the conquest. If he didn't connect with a sub, he simply moved on to the next one. Austin had never enjoyed playing fast and loose with a sub's emotions, and he damned well wasn't going to take any chances with the woman he was convinced was his mate.

Mine. Mate. With two simple words, he'd let Israel know this woman was his and all the rules were new. Reaching down, Austin trailed his fingers through the soaked folds of her labia. Swirling the tip of one finger in a lazy circle around her clit, he smiled down into her bright green eyes. Watching each and every one of her reactions was quickly becoming his new favorite pastime.

"So wet for me. When was the last time you had sex, *Little Star*?" He wasn't sure what surprised her more, the question or the term of endearment. The moniker suited her perfectly—she shimmered like the brightest star in the sky, and he looked forward to discovering all the ways to make her sparkle without the use of magic.

"Little Star? Is that a reference to what happened earlier at the club?"

He knew she'd hoped they had moved past that, but she'd soon learn he couldn't be distracted. Austin spent years rebuilding his parent's failing business—tenacity was just one of the skills he'd relied on. The experience taught him a number of valuable and hard-earned lessons, but chief among those was to stay focused on his goal.

"Yes, but we'll discuss that later." *After we spin you up a couple of times, you'll be willing to tell us anything we want to know if it will earn you the orgasm your sweet body will be craving as if your life depended on it.*

"Sex, Charlotte? When was the last time a man slipped his cock between these slick folds before shoving balls deep in your sweet body?" Pushing his finger just inside the opening of her vagina, he felt her muscles quiver as they squeezed him with surprising strength. When her eyes closed and her breathing sped up, he wondered when she'd last gotten off—he was shocked by how quickly she responded to his touch.

"Sex? Like real sex?"

Real sex? Is there another option?

Not for me, but I think she means as opposed to oral or masturbation.

"Yes, Charlotte, *real sex.* Sex where a man slides his cock inside your slick heat before pulling back, only to shove himself in again. Sex where your body takes over, silencing your mind. Now, stop stalling and answer the question." The longer she waited to answer, the more curious he became.

"Well, I haven't actually... I've been sort of busy."

Too busy to have sex? Austin knew she was younger than his thirty-one years, but she was certainly old enough to have been sexually active.

"While I'm not sure busy is a reasonable explanation, I'm more pleased than you can possibly know that I don't have to kill anyone for touching what's mine." He smiled, hoping to take some of the sting out of his words. "Knowing you're prepared to give me such a precious gift is humbling, and I promise to make it an experience you'll never regret. We're going to go slow, sweetheart— probably slower than you'll want to, but it's important you're properly prepared. It will be our pleasure to make certain your slick pussy is ready. We begin as we intend to go; spread your legs further apart. I'm going to fuck you with my fingers; you have permission to come whenever you're ready."

Austin hadn't planned to push her this fast, but if he didn't get some part of himself inside her, his wolf was going to break free, and Charlotte wasn't ready for that yet. She may have seen them shift from a distance, but up close and personal was going to be something entirely different. He couldn't help wondering if Charlotte would experience her own change once he claimed her—as a magical, the chances were much higher she'd become a shifter as well. If she made the change, he'd test her exhibitionist kink in an outdoor ceremony, announcing their mating to the rest of the pack. Great Goddess, just thinking about fucking her in wolf form at the center of a sacred circle made his cock throb with the need to claim her in every way possible.

Pushing his finger in until he encountered the thin

membrane barrier of her innocence, Austin pulled back before sliding in again.

"We're going to keep this shallow, that precious barrier will stay in place until my cock claims it." He didn't need deep penetration to send her over. Her clit was perfectly pearled and peeking out from under its hood, and each time he circled the little bundle of nerves, he felt a fresh wash of cream coat his fingers. Oh yeah, she was so responsive, he could spend hours playing with her. Every breath he took cemented his belief she belonged to him. Her scent was imprinting itself on him in the most primitive way possible. Centuries of shifters mating, the history now a part of his DNA, was all coming to fruition.

Sensing how close she was, Israel stepped behind Charlotte. Wrapping an arm around her torso, he was already in place when her knees folded out from under her. The smile on his brother's face was one of pure carnal desire—Israel would enjoy his time as their third, but he would never be a threat to Austin's claim on his mate.

"Oh, Goddess, it feels so good. I can't... Why is this so different from what I..."

Austin needed a closer connection and knew one way to strengthen their ties was to imprint her DNA into his system. Switching hands, Austin sucked his cream-soaked fingers into his mouth and felt his cock pulse with the need to sink in balls deep. Instantly, he felt their connection strengthen in small increments. Austin couldn't hear her yet, but he was able to sense her emotions. Overwhelming desire wafted through his mind, and the primal urge to claim his mate became a gnawing need.

"So different from what, Little Star?" His question was

rasped out in a voice he barely recognized. Austin was reasonably certain he knew what she meant, but Charlotte needed to learn to be completely transparent concerning her feelings.

"Your fingers know my body better than my own. I don't know how, but it's true. The pleasure is overwhelming."

Her words were airy, and he sensed she was genuinely confused. One of the joys of introducing Charlotte to the D/s lifestyle was showing her as her Dom and mate, he would indeed know far more about her sweet body than she ever could.

"I watch you, Charlotte. I study your reactions—the way your eyes dilate, the hitches in your breathing, and the lovely rose flush of arousal spreading from between your lush breasts, radiating out in all directions." A full body shudder racked her from head to toe, the accompanying moan the sweetest sound he'd heard in a long time. "Brother, I'll bet our sweet sub has a tight rosette. Check and see if I'm right. I'll bet we can send her over in under ten seconds."

Charlotte gasped as the tip of Israel's finger rimmed her anus. Using her body's natural lubrication, he pushed past the tight ring of muscles, and Charlotte's mind blanked. She fell forward as far as Israel's hold allowed, and thankfully, it put her plump lips in the perfect position for Austin to seal in her scream as she unraveled. The wash of cream over his fingers was hotter than hell and knowing they'd given her the first of many orgasms she'd experience at their hands was satisfying as hell.

"Fuck me, you are beautiful when you come, Little

Star. Now for that soak in the tub."

"I... I need a minute to make sure my legs are going to hold me up." She swayed, but thankfully, Israel still had one arm wrapped around her waist. When Austin growled, Israel swept her up into his arms.

"An emergency room visit doesn't sound like a good way to spend the rest of our night. I'd much rather play with you. Let's get you settled while big brother makes a couple of calls."

Austin stood rooted in place as Israel made his way down the long hall to the master suite. They'd played together often, so the routine wasn't unfamiliar—but something about this didn't feel right. Charlotte was *his* mate, and letting his brother care for her didn't feel right.

Sucking in a deep breath, Austin tried to clear the fog of frustration from his mind. He pushed aside the underlying feeling of envy, knowing Israel was providing the care he felt entitled to. Damn. He'd never been jealous of any woman they'd shared, but this felt different. Pushing the confusion aside, Austin pulled his phone from his pocket and emailed the spa staff with very specific instructions.

Next, he ordered several toys from his favorite kink store, paying an exorbitant fee for personal delivery first thing in the morning. The set of anal toys would stretch her rear hole, ensuring they could have a true ménage before Austin took her home on Sunday. Hell, was he going to be able to let her go? What if she didn't want to be his mate and sub? He persuaded people to his way of thinking all the time, but these were decisions she needed to make of her own free-will. Safe, sane, and consensual were the guiding tenants of the D/s lifestyle, and he'd always felt they applied to mating in the shifter world as well.

Staring into the fire, Austin wondered how his life had changed so much in the past few hours, yet he still felt as though things were far from settled. He needed to find out about her magical background. There was something about the entire situation that seemed far too coincidental. What were the odds a magical would make her way into his office as his Administrative Assistant?

"I agree she is hiding something, but it doesn't feel malevolent." Austin turned to see Israel reclining in a nearby chair. "I can't remember the last time anyone was able to enter a room without you knowing."

Israel was right, he'd already learned to be cautious before he learned to shift. Their dad had emphasized their lives depended on staying in the shadows and being self-aware. Rubbing his hand over his face, Austin shook his head.

"Me either. I can see why packs close ranks around their newly mated members." Hell, if he was this distracted before he claimed Charlotte, what would it be like after? No wonder new mates were isolated for several weeks—and the pack Alpha would be particularly vulnerable. "I want to know what she's hiding." It wouldn't change the fact he recognized her as his mate—he could only hope it wasn't something he couldn't live with.

Chapter Four

C HARLOTTE TRIED TO relax in the enormous tub, but her mind was still spinning at warp speed. The past couple of hours had been an emotional roller coaster, and it didn't sound as if she was going to find the ride's exit anytime soon. Damn it, why hadn't she pushed to have everything in place sooner. She still had some research to do before making her case to Austin. If the project she knew he was considering became a reality, her family and friends would lose everything. Oil exploration had been pushing the boundaries of their homeland for years, but this would be the final blow. Tears slipped free despite her valiant effort to hold them back.

"Enjoy the weekend, Charley. There is still time to figure out a way everyone can win. Cedar Bayou still belongs to the lost magicals... at least for now." Whispering the words to herself, Charlotte wished desire alone was enough to make her dream come true.

AUSTIN WATCHED CHARLOTTE in what he knew was a rare unguarded moment. She hadn't noticed him in the reflection of the mirrors. Watching the tears streak down her pale cheeks brought a tidal wave of protectiveness crashing to the surface. As the oldest, Austin had always felt responsible for his siblings, but this was something so much more—Goddess, he wasn't sure he could describe the gut-wrenching need he felt to pull her into his arms and soothe whatever had her so upset.

Listening as she gave herself a pep-talk, he frowned at the mention of Cedar Bayou. He recognized the name but didn't recall the details of the proposal he'd only given a passing glance. Making a mental note to ask Israel to check it out, he chuckled when his brother's voice floated through his mind.

On it. Leave it to Israel to be a step ahead of him at every turn. *Now would probably be a good time for me to re-negotiate our consulting contract, right?* Shaking his head at his brother's insolence, Austin refocused on Charlotte. Referring to herself as Charley had been a surprise. He'd never heard anyone else use the nickname and appreciated the glimpse at a side of her he hadn't seen previously.

Watching as she washed her hair, soaping and rinsing the long, auburn tresses three times before sniffing the strands, Austin felt a pang of guilt at the realization his earlier words had more of an impact than he'd known. After running her fingers through the strands, making sure the conditioner was evenly distributed, she drained the tub. Stepping gingerly over the slick rim of the bathtub, Charlotte moved to the shower.

Austin smiled as she stood inside the glass enclosure, studying the myriad of dials and switches. He'd spared no expense with the decadent enclosure. Heat lamps, side jets, rainfall heads, and waterfalls were all surrounded by lush greenery and smooth stone benches. Hidden speakers supplied music while the glass wall allowed a scenic panorama of the glittering lights of the city while shielding her from the view of the outside world. When he heard her muttering to herself about needing an engineering degree to take a shower, Austin stepped into the bathroom as he stripped out of his clothes.

"Let me help you."

Her gasp was quickly cut off when she turned to see him naked for the first time—well, the first time up close. Austin chuckled to himself when he realized she'd already seen him and Israel naked when she'd watched them shift. Knowing she'd enjoyed what many women would have been terrified to witness sent a surge of blood to his already rigid cock. Damn, he was going to split open if he didn't get some relief soon.

Setting the water temperature and dimming the lights, Austin stepped inside, crowding her against the glass. Turning her until her breasts were pressed against the cool glass, he smiled when she shivered.

"Let's see which sensation challenges you, shall we?" Pressing her more firmly against the glass, he pressed his palm against her lower back before slipping his fingers further south. "So slick and ready for me. Damn, you are a fucking dream come true, darlin'. How do your pretty nipples like the cool kiss of the glass?"

"Oh, Goddess. They are tight with just a little bit of an ache, but it's not enough. I need more… more something, but I'm not sure what."

"Do you ever play with these pretty pink nipples?" He

felt her tense against him and smiled. "Be honest, Charlotte. The first step in getting what you need is to be brave enough to be transparent." Even though he couldn't hear her thoughts yet, the wash of emotion rolling through her was unmistakable. She was terrified of being rejected, and while he was thrilled she wanted to please him, he didn't want her doing so out of fear. True submission lay in the sub's desire to please her Dom, his or her own pleasure deriving from the Masters. He saw her push her shoulders back and take a deep breath before meeting his eyes in the glass's reflection.

"I've tried, but it was never like what I'd read about in my books. Those women must have much more sensitive breasts… or maybe I wasn't doing it right." The pink stain on her cheeks let him know the admission had cost her, but he wasn't going to let it stand in his way.

"Spread your legs for me, baby." When she complied, Austin slid his hand between their water-slicked bodies, slipping two fingers between her folds, stroking from her clit to her ass. The slow teasing passes weren't enough to push her over, but those snippets of time were seeped in anticipation, certainly rocking her closer to the edge.

"I think Israel and I can help you find that edge, Little Star. We'll try a few things when we get to the playroom and see what you like." Grabbing the handheld showerhead, he began rinsing the conditioner from her hair, running his fingers through the silken strands, looking forward to seeing them spread over his thighs as his cock disappeared between her lush lips. When his cock bounced against her ass, he watched her reflection in the glass, pleased to see her eyes widen before clouding with lust.

"Do you need me to... umm... well, help you?" Her bright eyes reflected her uncertainty, and it warmed his heart to know she'd offered herself to him.

"Help me? How do you want to help me, darlin'?" He knew what she was asking, but he also sensed she had no idea what she was offering. Amazed at her lack of experience, he might have been tempted to let her try if he hadn't been worried she might drown before admitting her innocence.

"Don't men like it when women suck on their cocks? All the books talk about blow jobs, and I thought maybe you could... well, maybe I could do that for you since you gave me such a mind-numbing orgasm earlier." Oh, she thought they were going to keep score? That was something they needed to clear up right away.

"Don't bother keeping a tally, Charlotte, it's a waste of your time. Israel and I gain pleasure from seeing yours. Watching you splinter apart as you come is my new favorite pastime. There may be times when I take my pleasure without consideration for yours, but those will be rare. Orgasm denial is not my preferred method of punishment." A shiver of fear moved up her spine, and he shook his head. "We haven't talked about hard and soft limits yet but let me tell you mine—perhaps it will put your mind at ease." Pulling her back into his arms, he relished how perfectly she fit against him.

"Nothing that exposes us to blood or breaks the skin." Although he'd make an exception to this when he claimed her. "No permanent marks to your beautiful skin." Okay, this was going to be another exception because the small puncture wounds would leave a faint scar intended to let other shifters know she'd been claimed. It didn't matter that her scent would forever be altered, the small imperfections on the surface of her skin would be a visible reminder he looked forward to seeing beneath his collar.

"Is there anything you'd like to add?"

"I don't want to be humiliated or locked in a cage." Austin quirked a brow, surprised at how quickly she'd answered. He wondered if either of those was a trigger, and her response about humiliation went a long way to explain her concern when he'd suggested a long soak in the tub.

"I don't believe in humiliating submissives, Little Star." He would never begrudge anyone else their kink, but it wasn't anything he'd even consider. It was against everything he believed in. His mom always emphasized the Law of Attraction, and Austin felt applying that universal principle to his business dealings was one of the reasons he was so successful. He would never consider hurting his mate in such a way.

"I don't believe in subjecting anyone to degradation." He'd built his business reputation on treating associates and employees with respect. "I have never used a cage with a submissive, and as a shifter, the thought sends ice into my blood. Tell me why it's important to you." If he hadn't been studying every nuance of her body language, he'd have missed the subtle shudder that moved up her spine. "Are you claustrophobic, Little Star?"

"Just with cages. They terrify me." He waited for her to finish because it was easy to see there was more to the story. Her eyes darted around the shower as if reassuring herself she could escape the glass and stone enclosure.

Grabbing the soap and what his sisters called a bath scrunchie, Austin turned Charlotte back to the glass and began washing her back. He hoped she'd feel more comfortable talking about why cages frightened her so much if she didn't have to look him in the eye. He was still able to see her reflection in the glass, but with her gaze locked on the city lights beyond, she was able to avoid looking at him directly.

"I was locked in a cage once a long time ago. My parents had warned me over and over to be careful. I was forbidden to shimmer outside our small house, but I was rebellious, and it was hard to practice all the… things I was learning." She sighed, and Austin felt her trying to shore up her resolve to hold tightly to the secrets she'd carried since she started to work for him. Squatting behind her, Austin nudged her legs further apart and murmured his approval when she didn't hesitate. Smoothing the soapy puff over her legs, he teased the insides of her thighs.

"Talk to me, Little Star. I need to know what your triggers are if I'm going to avoid them. This is clearly a huge issue, and as much as I enjoy bondage, scaring you is the last thing I want to do." Leaning forward, he bit down hard enough on her ass cheek to elicit a squeak of surprise. "I'm looking forward to shackling you to the St. Andrew's cross, but I want it to be for pleasure, not punishment."

Pushing his calloused fingers between the folds of her labia, he smiled when he found them coated with her cream. Austin's subtle warning wasn't lost on Charlotte if her soaked sex was any indication.

"My family is magical, but I seem to have more skills than either of my parents. I've always felt a certain responsibility because the Great Goddess gave me so much."

"But it's come at a huge personal cost, hasn't it, darlin'?" He understood more than she could ever know. He'd taken on a failing family business far too young when a drunk driver crossed the center line, killing his parents. Throwing himself into rebuilding what his dad had never taken seriously became an obsession. He'd felt the crushing weight of that responsibility each and every day. "I understand how overwhelming family responsibilities can be." Sensing she'd said all she was going to, for now, Austin stood and leaned over her shoulder to whisper in her ear.

"I hope you'll trust me with the rest of your story soon. For now, I want you to remember your safe words and when you are supposed to use them. Israel and I will both be watching you carefully, but since the three of us haven't played together before tonight, it's possible we'd miss a sign of distress. It's your responsibility to speak up if you're getting uncomfortable or feel uncertain you'll be able to handle what we're going to do. For tonight, we'll tell you what's coming, but I'm warning you now, we won't always share what we have planned. We won't blindfold you tonight, but rest assured, it's in your future." Austin loved taking away a sub's ability to see, forcing her to rely on her other senses, intensifying their reactions to his touch. He enjoyed watching them flush at even the most faintly murmured words of praise.

Pulling her from the shower, Austin wasn't surprised to see Israel standing just outside. Tossing a warm towel to Austin, his brother pulled Charlotte close, enclosing her in another bath sheet from the nearby warmer.

"Oh God, you are going to spoil me."

Oh, yes, indeed, my sweet mate. I have every intention of drowning you in decadent pleasure. Watching a sub he'd picked up at Prairie Winds or Dark Desires snuggle against Israel had never bothered Austin before, but seeing Charlotte's face pressed against his brother's chest had his wolf clamoring for freedom. *Mine!*

May have to up your game, brother.

Israel's teasing pulled him back from the edge. Shaking his head as he turned to hide his smile, Austin wondered how he was going to be able to stay focused once they got her into the playroom. With the various scents of the club washed from her pale ivory skin, his senses were overwhelmed with the need coming off her in waves.

Austin's cock pulsed against his belly when she turned to him. Her resolve to learn about the lifestyle was appealing, but knowing it was couched in innocence reinforced his respect for her courage. Standing naked in front of two Dominants with years of sexual experience had to be damned intimidating. His little mate might be made of stronger stuff than he knew. Knowing she'd survived being locked in a cage impressed Austin as much as knowing she'd had to enraged him.

Taking the comb from her hand, Austin wrapped his large hand around her wrist and led her into the sitting area of the master suite. He'd pulled on a faded pair of jeans, zipping them carefully over his erection without bothering with the top button. Watching her eyes trace over his chest before following the trail of dark hair arrowing south fed his ego.

"You keep looking at me like that, and we won't make it to the playroom, darlin'." Her eyes jerked up to meet

Austin's as her face flushed a deep scarlet.

Settling on the loveseat his designer had sworn fit perfectly in front of the glass and marble gas fire line, Austin pulled Charlotte in front of him. Smiling to himself, Austin remembered the look on Asia's face when she'd seen the room's focal point. His sister had immediately insisted on a larger version in the outdoor living area the two of them created. Wrapping his large hand around her delicate wrist, Austin pulled Charlotte into position, settling her naked form between his legs and began untangling her hair.

"I can do that." When she turned to take the comb, he shook his head and straightened her shoulders.

"I'm sure you can." Once he'd finished, Austin braided the long locks, tying it off with a strip of leather Israel handed him. "We don't want to risk your hair getting caught in any of the equipment."

"Nor will we allow you to use it as a shield to hide behind, sweet Charlotte. We need to be able to see those bright green eyes so we can gauge how things are going. You are far too important to risk." Israel's indulgent smile told Austin the other man had already relegated her to the friends with benefits category. The wave of relief moving through him was humbling.

"Let's move to the playroom. I'm looking forward to seeing your fair skin sporting stripes from Israel's flogger." Her quick indrawn breath as he led her down the hall made Austin wish he already knew all her secrets so he could spend the weekend playing freely with her, instead of worrying about stepping on a mine. Stopping in front of the locked door, Austin smiled. Damn, he loved seeing the mixture of anticipation and apprehension in her eyes.

Taking a minute to commit this moment to memory, Austin made a mental note to ask his brother, Bronx, to photograph Charlotte—better yet, he'd ask his kid brother for a camera recommendation and take the shots himself. Car dealerships might be Bronx Adler's career, but photography was his passion.

"Once we step through this door, you are not allowed to speak unless it's to use one of your safe words or answer a direct question." She trembled in his hold, and he drew her full attention, gripping her chin with his fingers. "Do not hesitate to use yellow if you have questions or concerns. There is no shame in asking for a moment to get yourself in the right frame of mind. This is about your pleasure. Don't forget that."

Stepping through the door ahead of Charlotte, Austin moved to the side so he could watch her reactions as she took in the playroom he'd spent an enormous amount of money making it into every Dom's dream space. Charlotte's eyes took in the room in a slow perusal from left to right. He saw her breathing hitch when her gaze moved to the armoires and display cabinets. If she was scandalized by the floggers and paddles, he wondered what she'd think if she could see the array of toys hidden from view in the drawers. Austin was meticulous about safety, so plugs and vibrators were only used once before being replaced.

Looking around, Austin tried to see the space from Charlotte's point of view and was surprised at how intimidating it might appear to an inexperienced submissive. The steel rails on the ceiling were used to move equipment and enable bondage in numerous locations giving the large space an industrial feel. He hadn't wanted the area to look like a medieval dungeon. Since shifters had a long history of being imprisoned and tortured, Austin felt no need to expose his soul to the negativity. Walking into clubs around the world where the dungeon theme was predominant always made his chest ache, knowing how many of his kind had died in similar circumstances just because they were different.

Chapter Five

CHARLOTTE SHIVERED WHEN Austin took the towel Israel had wrapped her in after the shower they'd shared. The room was intimidating, more because it was filled with equipment she couldn't identify than the warehouse feel of the sizable space. The oversized bed along the back wall with its small spotlights drew her eye. Where the hell did anyone find a bed that large? *Bet they don't sell those sheets at Walmart.*

Rolling her eyes at her own distraction, Charley let her gaze sweep over the various pieces of equipment, recognizing several from descriptions in her erotic romance novels. The St. Andrew's Cross was a lot larger than she'd imagined one would be, and the cabinet beside it displaying a plethora of impact toys made her breath hitch. Suddenly conscientious of her inexperience, Charlotte wrapped her arms around herself.

"Arms at your sides, Charlotte. You are lovely and have no reason to hide what is ours to enjoy."

Israel had been letting Austin take the lead, so his command startled her. Dropping her arms to her sides, she had to concentrate on leaving them in place when her nipples drew up into even tighter buds. Charlotte hadn't identified all the Adlers' magical gifts, but she knew Austin had the mystical ability to compel compliance and was pleased he hadn't used it on her. As a magical herself, she would recognize his use of the gift even if she wasn't able to resist the command.

"The correct response is 'Yes, Sir.'" Israel's words were emphasized by a stinging slap to her bare ass.

He'd obviously known she'd become lost in her own thoughts. Charlotte spent so much time away from her family after leaving home, she'd learned to escape the loneliness by retreating into her mind. She'd thrown herself into her work, long hours and practicing her magic every day kept most of the morose feelings at bay. Sighing to herself, Charlotte wondered if she would ever feel like she belonged in the city. She missed the bayou and all the medicinal plants available around every turn.

Watching Austin move across the room to a metal tray mounted on tall legs with wheels, Charlotte began worrying her hands in front of her. Israel snarled something under his breath Charlotte wasn't able to hear before he pulled her in front of the St. Andrew's Cross.

"It's time to get you out of your own head, sweet girl. I'm not sure I've ever met a sub more in need of a good flogging." It was the first time she'd heard frustration in Israel's tone, and it sent unease skittering up her spine. Without realizing it was happening, the air around her started to sparkle. "Don't you fucking dare." Everything seemed to happen in slow motion from that point. Israel's growled words, startled her enough she reflexively jumped back. Her sudden movement had her crashing into the cart Austin was pushing toward them, sending everything he'd painstakingly laid out careening to the dark marble floor.

The shattering of glass made the air shimmer around her again, but Austin's curse drew her attention before Israel could chastise her a second time. Since she was barefoot, Charlotte stood rooted in place. Grabbing a hand towel, Austin wrapped the white cotton around his hand before picking her up and moving her to what looked like the medical table at her gynecologist's office. Seeing blood soak through the towel, Charlotte reached for his hand.

"Let me see." Her plea was met with Austin's frown, but he unwrapped the towel to show her a deep cut slashed over his palm. Without saying anything, Charlotte placed her palm over his, focusing her attention on healing the gash. The familiar heat began radiating down her arm, and she smiled when she heard him gasp.

"Holy fucking hell." Austin's eyes widened, and she felt him begin pulling back.

"Hold still, please." Charlotte tightened her hold on his hand, recentering the restorative energy she'd practiced since discovering she was a healer. Concentrating the powerful energy, she felt the telltale searing over her own palm a heartbeat before seeing the first drop of her blood fall, splashing silently against the dark marble. By the time Austin realized what she'd done, his hand looked as if it had never been cut.

"Damn it, Charlotte, what have you done?" Glass crunched under his feet when he stalked across the room to retrieve another towel, but by the time he returned, the cut on her own hand was already mending. "Good Goddess." Austin's words were spoken with reverence, and she realized he'd stopped dead in his tracks. He looked from her to his brother who was staring at her with his mouth hanging open.

"You know, as shifters, we heal at an accelerated rate, right?" This time, Israel's tone was teasing rather than tinged with frustration. "He'd have been good as new in an hour or so. Although I have to admit, that was damned impressive."

Austin was staring at her like she'd sprouted a second head. *Fuck a furry fairy, what have I done?*

Charlotte knew exactly what happened. She'd reacted in emotion rather than using her head. Fudgesicles, this was precisely the sort of thing that had gotten her in trouble so many times as a kid. It had been years since she'd made such a bold mistake. Taking a deep breath before expelling it slowly, Charlotte nodded.

"Yes. I wasn't thinking." Shifting her attention to Austin, she hoped the small smile she gave him reached her eyes. "I'm sorry about the mess. If you bring my shoes, I'll help you clean up before I go." He didn't respond immediately... instead, he tilted his head to the side, watching her for what seemed an eternity.

"Go? Were you given permission to leave, Little Star?" When she shook her head slowly, he raised a brow and waited. It took her several seconds to remember Israel's earlier instruction.

"No, Sir." His nod was almost too subtle to notice, but the small bit of approval started an avalanche of emotion thundering through her. Why did his approval mean so much more in this setting than it did at work? Hell, she'd gone toe-to-toe with him more than once during the short time she'd worked at Adler Oil.

"Are you saying your safe word?" Sliding his feet further apart, Austin crossed his arms over his chest as he waited for her to respond.

Biting her lip, Charlotte fought the urge to mutter the damned word just because the arrogant man believed she wouldn't, but the truth was, she wanted to learn what they could teach her. Damn it, she'd waited years for this moment, and she didn't want to give up when the opportunity was standing right in front of her.

And you need his help, too, Charley. Don't forget why you're here. Unfortunately, the reason she'd agreed to spend the night in Austin's playroom had nothing to do with Cedar Bayou.

ISRAEL WASN'T SURE he'd have believed it if he hadn't seen it for himself. Not only could Charlotte shimmer her pretty ass into invisibility, but she'd also just healed a gash on Austin's hand. The injury had appeared for less than a minute on her own hand before healing at a faster rate than any shifter he'd ever seen. He'd dealt with many individuals with magical abilities, but this was the first time he'd seen a healer take an injury themselves. She might believe she'd acted out of nothing but impulsivity, but he knew better.

Charlotte had acted out of love. Israel didn't believe she was in love with Austin, at least not yet, but her actions had been motivated by an altruistic form of love—something Israel hadn't witnessed in a long time. Sure, he saw his brothers and sisters do things from a place of love, but seeing an outsider jump to his brother's aid with no thought to what it would cost her personally was humbling.

"How old were you when you found out you could heal others?" She looked up at Israel and smiled, but he could see this wasn't a conversation she wanted to have. "I promise to hold most of my questions until tomorrow morning, sweetness, but I want honest answers to the few I ask tonight." Charlotte nodded and took a deep breath.

"My parents made the discovery right before my third birthday. My dad cut his leg while using a chain saw, and when I saw my mother panic, I rushed to his side to help him hold the wound closed." Charlotte paused long enough, Israel wondered if she could continue or leave them to the obvious conclusion. "My father's relief was immediate but short-lived. When he and mom saw blood running down my leg, they were horrified." Grinning, Charlotte shrugged.

"I've been told once they saw I was healing so quickly, they calmed down, but some of the people who were there have told me my mom was confined to bed for days afterward." *She started traveling a lot after that, I was just too much for her.* Neither Israel nor Austin said anything. They waited in silence for her to finish her story. What she hadn't said out loud was every bit as important as what she'd shared, and Israel continued listening on both levels.

"I doubt I have to explain how significant the implications were. We had to move several times because people would line up outside our house so they could catch me whenever I ventured outside. I was homeschooled, but it was torture being stuck inside all the time."

Looking at his brother, Israel saw his tortured expression. No doubt he felt the intense anxiety coming off Charlotte in waves as strongly as Israel did. *It's time to end this for now. Let's give your mate something else to think about, shall we?*

Hell, yes. I know this discussion isn't finished, but she's had a rough night and deserves a break.

Israel agreed. Wrapping his hand around her slender wrist, Austin led her past the St. Andrew's Cross she'd looked at it with curiosity dancing in her green eyes. Stopping in front of the frame, Austin gave her time to look over the equipment before speaking.

"We call this *the frame* for obvious reasons. Since Austin and I will both be playing with you, it's a better choice than the St. Andrew's Cross. It gives us both access to almost every sweet inch of your tempting body." Pausing to give her a chance to ask questions, he fought to hold back his grin when her gaze finally moved to his.

"I can see why you might prefer this. Does the whole thing tilt?"

Israel raised his brow, waiting for her to respond appropriately. He knew Austin wanted to begin as they intended to go, but he could also sense the fog filling his brother's mind. *Hell, this is the reason I don't ever intend to mate—it seriously fucks you up.*

"Sir. Does the whole thing tilt, Sir?" Giving her a nod of approval, he pointed to one side of the apparatus.

"Yes, it does. A Dom can lock the frame in place at any point on the 360-degree circle, leaving the submissive completely open and available to whatever he or she has planned." Israel knew his brother planned to fuck Charlotte, but Austin wouldn't want the memory of her first time linked to a piece of kink equipment. "I'm going to secure you to the frame, but we won't be using the waist strap since we won't be tilting you." Giving her a lecherous grin, Israel waited for a few beats before adding, "This time."

Israel talked to Charlotte the entire time he was cuffing her inside the frame, pleased to see the rosy flush of arousal moving over her torso. He'd be using the softest flogger in his brother's cabinet for two reasons. Even though it wasn't perfect for a newbie, Israel could easily adjust the strokes to ensure Charlotte wasn't pushed too far, but the most important reason was the deerskin implement was new. Knowing his oldest brother as well as he did, Israel knew he'd never allow a toy to touch his mate if it had been used on another sub. *Hell, I'll just empty out big brother's bag and help him out.*

You're a regular fucking prince among men.

Israel gave his brother a knowing grin at the caustic response before stepping behind Charlotte, drawing the supple strips of deer hide over her shoulders, up and down her arms in a continuous looping pattern. He let the predictability of his move lure her into a semi-hypnotic state before he started flogging her. Israel was pleased to see how quickly the tension melted from her muscles, her head rolling back on her shoulders.

"How does it feel, Little Star?"

Austin's voice was already rough with lust Israel wasn't used to hearing, and they'd barely begun playing with Charlotte. Israel focused on using the flogger to tease her blood to the surface to avoid leaving any marks once he intensified the strokes.

"Warm. It feels like my entire back half is being warmed by the summer sun breaking through the dense foliage of the bayou." Israel gave her ass a sharp blow, eliciting a gasp. "Sir." Looking over her shoulder, Israel saw his brother's indulgent smile.

"Perfect, Charlotte. I love hearing that word cross your lips and look forward to the day when you call me Master." Israel ramped up the intensity of the flogger's strokes, happy when the scent of Charlotte's arousal filled the vast open space. Hell, his cock was already pressing against his zipper with enough pressure to give it a permanent tattoo. *She's holding back, brother.*

Up the stakes. My sweet mate needs more, and I think we need to help her out.

Chapter Six

AUSTIN WATCHED CHARLOTTE fall deeper and deeper into a submissive mindset as Israel flogged her upper back, ass, and thighs. The steady thudding of the flogger falls was almost hypnotic, and seeing her response was the most erotic thing he'd ever witnessed. Pulling a pair of alligator nipple clamps from his pocket, Austin held them up for her to see.

"Do you know what these are, darlin'?"

"Yes, Sir." Not the full response he'd expect from an experienced sub, but technically, she'd answered his question, so he'd let it slide.

"Tell me what you know about them while I play with your pink nipples." She gasped as he rolled both buds between his fingers. She didn't flinch when he pinched the peaks, and Austin was pleased Charlotte appeared to enjoy a small bite of pain.

"They're nipple clamps. I haven't seen them up close, but they are mentioned a lot in the books I've read." Her voice was filled with interest, need, and perhaps, a bit of apprehension.

I am going to check out her reading list. I hope like hell she used the same password on her phone as she did on her social media accounts.

Austin chuckled to himself because he remembered how frustrated Israel had been when he'd discovered Adler Oil's newest employee was using her last name and birthdate as a password on her personal accounts.

I thought you were annoyed she used the simple password. From your ranting and raving, I was convinced it was a crime against humanity. Hell, she hasn't ever posted anything other than cute animal videos, and you were raving about her account being hacked. Even Asia told you to lighten up, and she changes her passwords daily.

Well, now her lack of password paranoia serves my purpose. I'm an opportunist, sue me.

Letting his gaze drift back to Charlotte's face, Austin was surprised to find her studying him. Damn it, he and his brother had been so busy chatting, neither of them had noticed she was no longer immersed in their scene.

"Yellow." Austin was stunned. He'd never had a sub use a safe word, and the worst part was knowing he and Israel had missed all the signs. Fucking hell. He'd fucked up with the one woman who mattered the most, and he knew he would never forgive himself for the shattered look he saw in her eyes.

Israel tossed the flogger onto a nearby bench before kneeling to unfasten the cuffs around her ankles. Even though she'd only used the word to slow down the scene, they needed to get her out of the restraints before they talked. Austin pulled one of the soft subbie blankets from the warmer and wrapped it around her as soon as Israel unbuckled the last cuff.

"Come. We'll take this discussion to the living room."

Austin wanted to be sure Charlotte didn't feel any pressure and getting her out of the playroom was the first step in setting things right. When she stumbled, he realized he was walking much too fast for her to keep up without running. Turning to her, he started to apologize and saw tears trailing down her pale cheeks. Feeling as though someone had reached into his chest and yanked out his heart, Austin scooped her up into his arms.

"Goddess, I'm sorry, darlin'. I wanted everything to be perfect for you, and I'm not sure how I could have done any worse."

"It's not your fault you aren't attracted to me."

Austin barely heard his brother's whispered cursing over the roar of blood in his ears. Somehow, he managed to keep walking until he was able to sit on the sofa, settling her on his lap.

"You're wrong, baby. Thinking I'm not attracted to you is as far from the truth as it gets. I can't tell you how sorry I am for the way things went. To be honest, I'm not sure how everything went south so quickly." Austin hadn't had a scene go so far off track since his earliest days as a Dom. Israel hadn't immediately followed them out of the playroom, and Austin appreciated his brother giving him a minute alone with her.

"Tell me what happened to make you believe I'm not attracted to you." He could feel humiliation coming off her in waves, but he wasn't going to back away from this conversation—it was far too important.

"You and Israel were speaking telepathically." Austin wasn't sure why he was surprised she'd known they were communicating silently, but he was. Fucking hell, as a magical it only made sense, and he should have at least considered the possibility. "I wasn't able to hear much of it, but I know one of you was frustrated with me and the other thought it was funny."

Hear much of it? Great Goddess, what a cluster fuck. A fresh wave of tears filled her eyes and Austin wasn't sure he'd ever felt so helpless. Shifting her on his lap, so her knees were against his right side, Austin placed his hands along either side of her jaw, tilting her head back until she faced him. Brushing the tears from her cheeks with the pads of his thumbs, he vowed to make this night up to her—he wasn't sure how, but he'd find a way to turn this around.

"You heard me teasing my brother about his frustration with your passwords—something I believe he has already spoken to you about. The impetus for our conversation? Your reading list. You've mentioned the books you've read, and knowing what you've been reading would give us a lot of insight into what you've learned about the lifestyle. Anything we can learn about you and your prior experience will help us give you what you need."

"That is—if you are willing to give us another chance." Austin wasn't sure he'd ever heard his brother sound more remorseful.

"Tell us what you're thinking, Charlotte. If you want to go home tonight, I'll drive you myself, but I hope like hell you'll stay." Letting her walk away was going to kill him, but if she wanted to leave, he wouldn't stop her. Chewing on her bottom lip, Charlotte shifted her gaze from him to Israel, then back to him before focusing on her hands twisting in her lap.

"I'd like to stay… if you are serious about wanting me to. I know I'm not as slender or sophisticated as most of the women you spend time with—" He cut her off before she could continue.

"Be very careful, Charlotte. You are venturing into dangerous territory. I may feel guilty as hell about missing your earlier signs of distress, but I won't allow you to speak negatively about what I consider mine." Austin punctuated his words by pulling her into a rib-crushing hug.

"I don't know about you two, but I'm starving." Israel stepped in front of them, holding out his hand to Charlotte. "Come. I want to tend to the marks on your back while my brother makes us a snack."

Austin understood what his brother was trying to do, but that didn't make it any easier to let her go. Pushing to his feet, Austin was relieved to see Israel lead Charlotte to the breakfast bar—at least his sweet mate would still be in his line of sight even if she wasn't close enough to touch.

Hell, he wasn't hungry for anything but her. What the hell was he going to throw on a plate that would look like he'd actually taken an interest in feeding them? Pulling open the refrigerator door with enough force to rock the commercial grade appliance, Austin sent up a silent prayer of thanks when he saw a plate of sandwiches his house-keeper must have left to help him get through the weekend. Mildred Kipling had worked for his parents before moving in with him. He had no idea how old the little spitfire was—hell, she'd looked exactly the same his entire life.

Mildred was a member of their pack, but he rarely saw her outside the penthouse. When he'd offered to build her a place of her own a few floors down, she politely accepted then refused to cash her checks for several months. Shaking his head at the memory, Austin fought the urge to smile at the memory of their confrontation. Mildred had been adamant she should shoulder some of the cost of her apartment, and he'd been equally committed to ensuring she was paid for the work she did every day, so he'd simply started depositing her checks directly into her bank account.

Setting the plate of sandwiches on the counter, Austin watched Israel trace several scarlet stripes on Charlotte's upper back. Austin knew the marks would be gone before morning, but he appreciated Israel checking her level of discomfort. There was no reason for Charlotte to experience any physical discomfort after the emotional toll their earlier inattention had wrought. Israel pulled the subbie blanket further down so he could check the lash stipes covering her ass and thighs. Looking away from the sight of his brother's hands on his mate's bare ass, Austin fisted his own hands at his side in an attempt to hold back his wolf.

Calm the fuck down, I'm not groping her—although the thought holds a considerable amount of appeal. "The marks will be gone before morning, so I don't think you'll scandalize the spa staff."

"Kent is sending two of the estheticians from the club's spa. He swears Tobi and Gracie are staffing geniuses." Shrugging when Israel cast him a questioning look, he added, "For what it's worth, Cameron Barnes claims his turnover in the Forum Shops is so low, he'd like to bring the women in to consult when he hires staff for other club positions. Something about their uncanny ability to spot what they call candy-ass posers. Whatever the fuck that means." Charlotte's snort of laughter was music to his ears. Grinning at her, he caught himself chuckling as well.

"Tobi is a force of nature. She's a bundle of brilliance hiding behind the disconnected persona. But I'm telling you, nothing could be further from the truth. I'm not sure I've ever met anyone as forward thinking when it comes to business. Their Forum Shops idea is being replicated in clubs all over the world even though they refuse to travel outside the continental United States without one of their husbands going along. I'm not sure whose idea that is, but I'm glad they take their safety seriously. I've become very fond of them." Charlotte took a deep breath and sighed. "Tobi and Gracie are unstoppable because they are both driven to succeed despite seeing the path to success from completely different angles. They are the perfect example of the expression... the whole is greater than the sum of its parts."

Austin stared at Charlotte in disbelief. She'd just spoken more at one time than he'd ever heard her utter in the weeks she'd worked for him. Oh sure, she'd argued with him on occasion, but she'd always done so with a remarkable economy of words. Hell, there'd been days when he could count on two hands the number of words he'd heard her speak during the entire day.

"What?" Charlotte looked between the two of them, questions dancing in her bright green eyes.

"Well, for you, that was quite a dissertation, sweetness."

"Yes, indeed. I've never heard you say so much at one

time. For you, it was downright chatty. I've often wondered what you were like with your friends."

"You can't be friends with Tobi and not chatter... she doesn't allow it. Tobi doesn't suffer *quiet* very well, that's for sure." Charlotte's laughter lit her from the inside, totally transforming the attractive but far too serious woman he worked with into a raving beauty. Austin liked Tobi but hadn't spent any time talking to her one-on-one. He wondered what the West brothers' spirited wife would think when she found out her new friend was a magical mate to a shifter.

"Tobi is the least judgmental person I've ever met outside the magical community."

"Are you worried about what Tobi and Gracie will say when they learn you're a magical, Charlotte?"

Austin was relieved to hear Israel ask the question he'd asked himself a few minutes earlier. Moving around the long bar, Austin stepped behind Charlotte and wrapped her in his embrace. A shudder skittered up her spine before she relaxed, leaning back against him.

"Not really. I'd hate to lose their friendship, but I have enough to worry about without adding in things I can't control."

He couldn't argue with her logic even though he was more than a little curious about what she had to worry about.

They spent the next several minutes eating and chatting about how much they enjoyed the sense of comradery they felt at Prairie Winds. The casual chatter gave them all a chance to regroup, and Austin was pleased to see how easily they interacted. It was time well-spent, but now, it was time to move on.

"Israel is going to put away the sandwiches since this was his idea." Helping her from her seat, Austin unwrapped the blanket she'd covered herself with after Israel's inspection. "Come. I have plans for you, sweet sub." She shivered, but he knew it had nothing to do with the temperature of the room. "Lead the way, Little Star. I want to watch your exquisite ass sway as you walk down the hall." He heard Israel chuckle as he followed her down the hall.

"You're going to find out big brother is a bit of a voyeur, Charlotte."

Israel was right, watching others play was something Austin had always enjoyed. Hell, he'd gone to Dark Desires and Prairie Winds many times with no intention of playing himself. He loved watching a skilled sexual Dominant lead a submissive so deep into her own mind, she completely surrendered. Austin looked forward to seeing how Charlotte reacted to both voyeurism and exhibition. Nothing would change the fact she was his mate—but finding out their kinks aligned would be a huge bonus.

CHARLOTTE TOOK A deep breath, trying to calm her nerves. Walking down the long hall to Austin's bedroom seemed to take an eternity. Knowing he was looking at her bare ass as it jiggled was damned humbling. *The gym, Charley, you keep saying you'll go, then find every excuse possible to skip it. Might be time to commit to working out.*

"I can hear you, Charlotte, and I'll tattle if you don't

stop." The laughter in Israel's voice wafting down the hall didn't help her nerves at all. The sharp slap to her right ass cheek made her jump.

"Whatever self-deprecating nonsense you're allowing to float around in your head stops now, darlin'. You've already been warned once. Each infraction will result in double the number of swats your pretty ass receives, so I'd give the mathematics some careful consideration if I were you."

Spinning her around as soon as she stepped over the threshold, Austin pulled her into his arms and sealed his lips over her own. The kiss seared her from the top of her head to the tips of her toes. She'd expected sweet and coaxing, but what he delivered was passionate and dominant from the start. He fisted her hair, tugging with enough force to give her a small bite of pain that sent another rush of moisture to her already slick pussy. When she arched, trying to press her body against him, Austin tightened his hold in her hair. She recognized the warning for what it was and waited—even though she wanted nothing more than to find out if he wanted her as much as she wanted him.

"You press your sweet self against me, and I won't be responsible for what happens, Little Star. I'll take you hard and fast, and we both know you aren't ready for that—at least not yet." Charlotte's head knew he was right, but her body was playing from an entirely different sheet of music.

"Yes, Sir." Charlotte barely recognized her own voice. "It's just that... oh, wait. May I ask a question?"

"Charlotte, you are always allowed to ask questions outside formal scenes. High protocol isn't something I'd even consider until we know each other better."

"Do you ever let your sexual partners be in charge?" The question surprised him even though it probably shouldn't have.

"No, but probably not for the reason you're thinking. My wolf isn't able to turn off his alpha side. Even if the human side of my personality wanted to give it a shot, it wouldn't work."

She wasn't sure what prompted her to ask. Hell, she didn't want to be in charge, anyway. Maybe she wanted the security of knowing, in this one area, she didn't have to learn how to lead. Maybe there was a certain safety in knowing she could depend on someone else to take the reins in at least one small part of her life.

Charlotte had been forced to grow up at such a young age, she often felt as though she was responsible for everyone else's happiness… it was exhausting. Being able to put herself in someone else's care, even if only for a short time, would be a treat. Looking up, Charlotte noticed Austin seemed to be studying her.

"I don't think you want to be in charge in the bedroom, darlin'. You want to know you can take the leap of faith—that you can jump off the top of the mountain and feel absolutely certain I'll always be there to catch you."

Austin's response was so spot-on, it startled her, and she suspected her surprise reflected in her expression when he gave her a knowing smile.

"Don't look so surprised. I'm not a mind reader—well, at least not with you. But sweetness, you're a submissive, and there are certain aspects of your personality that are damned easy to read. If you just let go—let me lead you for just a little while—I will do everything I can to prove to you why putting yourself in my care is something you'll never regret."

"I'd like that. I want to be able to trust someone enough to push everything out of my mind."

"Close your eyes and open your mind. Stop using the energy to block—focus on receiving instead."

Nodding, Charlotte concentrated on dropping the shields she'd spent years holding in place. Feeling the shift within herself was staggering—with her mind open, the sexual pull between them ramped up exponentially.

"What you're feeling is only the beginning."

Charlotte wasn't sure what Austin meant, but she was anxious to find out. Her body was practically humming with need. Austin's hands skimmed up from her hips, following the contours of her body, his calloused palms smoothing over her waist before both hands lifted her breasts.

"Push your hands under mine." When she did as he directed, Austin used her fingers to roll her nipples into stiff peaks. "Lift your breasts and offer them to be me, Little Star."

When Austin stepped back, Charlotte felt a chill from the lost connection, the unwelcome sensation radiating from her core all the way to her toes. For several seconds, it was as if she'd plunged into a pool of frigid water. She would have sworn the air temperature dropped several degrees as chill bumps raced up her arms. Following his command, Charlotte lifted both breasts and pressed them together. Seeing his hard length pressed against his pants made her face flame with heat. Being able to turn on a man like Austin Adler was a huge confidence booster.

Now, if he'd just fuck me, maybe my brain would start functioning again.

Chapter Seven

"T HAT ISN'T HOW it's supposed to work, Charlotte. Our goal is to make certain your mind loses all sense of direction, and your brain stops working long enough that you know how sweet surrender can be." Israel's words were spoken over her shoulder, and he was impressed she'd seemed to sense his presence. He'd taken time to send out some additional feelers related to Cedar Bayou after straightening things in the kitchen.

One of the calls Israel made was to Asia, wanting to make sure she pulled together everything Adler Oil had on the Cedar Bayou project. The other call was to Luke Grayson, his sister, Brooklyn's fiancé. Why the two of them weren't already married was anybody's guess. If they didn't get married soon, Adler Oil was going to need to put Luke on the payroll, they called on him so often.

Luke promised to do *a bit of research*, which Israel knew translated to *hack into every available resource* and get back to him before the end of the weekend. When Israel inquired about Brooklyn, the other man laughed before informing him she was tied up at the moment before disconnecting. *Too much information, ass hole.*

"I am looking forward to finding out if I can have an

orgasm." The moment Charlotte blurted out the words, Israel felt her stiffen beneath the hands he was resting atop her shoulders.

"You've never orgasmed during masturbation?" Austin asked the question Israel would have asked if he hadn't been so shocked by her comment.

"No... but I didn't try very hard, to be honest. For many years, we lived in a tiny house at the edge of a bayou, and the walls were paper thin."

"But you've lived in your own apartment—wait—do you live alone?" Israel knew the minute he asked, she was sharing a place with several other people. He had a very clear vision of the small apartment and all the damned beds lined up along the walls. *What the hell is she doing with her money?*

"No. I have several... umm, roommates. It's cheaper for all of us this way, but there isn't much privacy."

Israel sensed there was more to the story, but he wanted to wait until the report came back from Luke before asking any more questions.

"Is that why you joined the club, Charlotte?"

"Yes, at least, that was part of the reason. I needed to find out if what I'd been reading about was real."

That damned reading list again. I want to know what's on that fucking list.

"Well, whatever the reason, I'm glad you were there. We wouldn't be standing here—at least, not yet—if you hadn't been at the club." *I still can't believe I didn't see the submissive hiding beneath the surface.*

What I want to know is how you didn't spot her as your mate. Israel thought back over the past few weeks, and the question practically answered itself. Austin had been traveling almost continually since Charlotte was hired. Most of their communication had been over the phone and via email. Once they got her between them, they'd be able to skirt the last of the barriers she'd erected. Israel pressed his chest against her shoulder blades as he smiled at Austin over her head.

You going to stand here all night or take what she is offering?

CHARLOTTE CAST A furtive glance at the bed and wondered how they were ever going to get there. Damn, she'd been waiting forever to lose her virginity, hell, it had almost become a curse. She hadn't dated much, but it hadn't taken many interactions with men to find out most were looking for a woman with experience. Austin made a sound that sounded suspiciously like a growl before picking her up and stalking across the room.

"You are making it damned hard for me to be a gentleman, Little Star." Tossing her on the bed, he grinned at her startled shriek. He was out of his faded jeans in record time and felt his ego inflate when her eyes widened at the sight of his erection.

"You're awfully... well, large. Are you sure this is going to work?"

He understood her trepidation and knew she wouldn't be convinced by his assurances. The only way to prove to his virgin mate he would indeed fit perfectly was to show her. By the time he began pushing his aching cock inside, she'd be begging him to take her.

"We're going to make certain you are ready, sweetness." Israel watched his brother move onto the bed, shouldering his way between Charlotte's thighs, pushing her legs so far apart, her face flushed with embarrassment. "He's going to make you come, Charlotte. Let Austin show you what it feels like to have a lover focused entirely on your pleasure." Austin began kissing his way up the insides of her thighs, moving from one side to the other. When Charlotte grabbed Israel's hand, he smiled down at her. "That's a good girl. You hang on to my hand and focus on the pleasure."

"Your skin is like warm silk, darlin'. I'm going to spend hours mapping every square inch with my hands and mouth. My mission this weekend is to learn every one of your sensitive spots—I want to know what will make you melt into a puddle and what pushes your boundaries."

Austin was lighting Charlotte up from the inside, and Israel was looking forward to watching as his brother claimed her innocence.

AUSTIN AND ISRAEL were going to kill her, it was just that simple. How much pleasure could one person take before they imploded? Charlotte was already racing toward the point of no return from Austin's kisses and nips along the insides of her thighs. Grabbing Israel's hand, she hoped he'd act as her anchor. She might not be experienced, but she could already feel herself spiraling out of control and needed something to tether her to the earth when her mind shattered.

Using his fingers to part her folds, Austin swiped his tongue over the sensitive flesh, and Charlotte's back arched off the bed.

"Oh, my Goddess. Please." She wasn't sure what she was begging for, hell, at this point she was functioning on instinct alone. Austin snarled and bit the inside of her leg with just enough force to make her yelp.

"If you want to come, you'll address me properly. We aren't observing high protocol, but that doesn't mean we've thrown all the rules out." Her mind was dissolving, and he was worried about being called Sir?

"Please, Sir. Master. Flying fairies, I'll call you anything you want me to if you'll keep doing... *that*."

"Oh, sweet Charlotte, you have so much to learn. Always quit while you're ahead."

What? Ahead? When was I ever ahead? Austin has been playing me like a secondhand fiddle he found at a flea market since he saw me shimmer at the club. I've never been ahead. I'm so far behind, he's lapped me at least once. Ahead? Not hardly! It wasn't until she realized neither man was moving, she worried she'd actually spoken the words aloud.

"Sir?" Her needy voice sounded like it belonged to someone else, but Charlotte didn't care. The only thing that mattered was finding the pleasure they'd promised her. "What? Oh, please, you promised, Master." Apparently, something she said turned the tide because Austin's mouth immediately descended, his tongue flicking over the tight bud of her clitoris peeking out from under its hood.

Charlotte's body was trembling so hard, she worried she might bounce right off the bed. Gripping Israel's hand tight enough to make her fingers numb, Charlotte finally gave in to the tidal wave of pleasure. Letting herself fall head first into a pool of bliss she wasn't sure had a bottom, her scream echoed off the walls, and when she heard Austin growl "Mine" against her quivering folds as the fog began to lift, the claim sent her head over heels into another release nearly as powerful as the first one.

"Open your eyes, Charlotte."

Oh, I don't think I can. It's too much work. My eyelids are too heavy, and I feel like a wet noodle. Maybe tomorrow… or Thursday.

"Sorry, darlin' but that's not going to work for me."

Fuck-a-dilly Circus. It was only a matter of time before I messed up and said stuff out loud.

"Come on, Little Star, open those pretty green eyes. I want to be able to see you as I push my cock through those quivering walls until I'm balls deep in your heat."

Charlotte finally managed to lift her eyelids, but the effort was draining, and she wasn't sure how long she would be able to keep them open. It took a Herculean effort to smile up into eyes so dark, her only clue where the pupils ended and the irises began was the golden hue ringing the edges. She'd seen the same color before in other shifters and knew his wolf was pushing back the human side. Looking down, Charlotte was surprised to see Austin had already rolled on a condom. Israel's hand moved over her breasts, giving each nipple a sharp pinch.

"Answer your Dom's question, sweetness."

Question? Oh, my stars and garters, keeping her eyes open was taking all her energy, there was no way she could manage her ears, too. *Nap first, then questions.* She heard Israel chuckle beside her but didn't have the energy to call him out.

"Let's see if I can't get my sweet mate to reengage."

Austin's comment had barely registered when she felt the tip of his penis press against her opening. *Wait, does he really think I'm his mate? Has he been to Australia recently? He probably means we're going to be friends... woohoo, friends with benefits. Holy cactus flowers, I gotta focus.*

Charlotte didn't often drink alcohol because it made her magic too unpredictable. It was the same feeling of not being totally in control, but this time, her body was singing the hallelujah chorus instead of some ditty about a hundred bottles of beer. Drinking wine on Galveston Island while eating seafood during a girls' night out, Charlotte had tried to send healing energy to a waiter who was suffering from a migraine.

Thank the great Goddess, Charlotte's aim had been as skewed as her magic because the heated energy she'd tried to send to the young man was clearly far too strong. The ball of fire bounced around the room, igniting everything it touched before landing on a stack of paper napkins and nearly burning the bistro to the ground. She'd fled with all the other patrons and thanked her lucky stars the small eatery's security camera had been one of the first things to go up in flames.

Austin chuckled as Israel burst out laughing, the light-hearted sounds pulling her back to the moment. Before she could bemoan speaking the entire story aloud, Austin pushed his tip up against the barrier of her innocence and paused.

"Take a deep breath, darlin'."

Opening her mouth to pull in a large gulp of air, Charlotte gasped instead when Austin pushed past the thin membrane. The flash of pain was gone before she fully registered the heated sensation.

"It only gets better from here, Little Star."

She was too stunned to do more than nod. Grateful Austin didn't demand she answer verbally, pleasure surged back to the surface, and within seconds, Austin made good on his promise.

"Oh, baby, if you think this is good, wait until we have you between us. A real ménage, with my brother in your sweet pussy and my cock, pushed deep in your ass."

Israel's words were punctuated by his brother's forward thrusts, and the combination was sending her racing toward another release. When Israel shifted away from her, Charlotte was shocked to see he was naked. Holy hell, when had he stripped? Kneeling beside her head, his cock bobbed just beyond her lips. When she reached for him, Israel shook his head.

"Oh, no you don't. If you wrap those soft fingers around me, I'll go off like a rocket." He lifted her arms over her head. "Hold on to the headboard and don't let go." When she did as he instructed, he pushed his tip against her lips, painting them with his pearly precum. "Open for me, Charlotte. Take me all the way to the back of your throat and swallow."

She did, humming as she swallowed around him, his strangled groan giving her immense pleasure. It was empowering to know she was able to do this for him.

"Holy fucking hell. Big brother, you're going to be playing solo if you don't distract your mate. Great Goddess, she has a devil blessed mouth."

There it was again, the reference to her as Austin's mate. In the back of her mind, Charlotte wondered if that explained her overwhelming attraction to him. Pushing aside everything but the pleasure, Charlotte refocused on the men introducing her to the world of ménage.

Charlotte relished the feel of his cock sliding over her tongue. She looked forward to mapping the veins and ridges of Austin's and Israel's cocks, using her fingers, then her tongue. Charlotte wanted to know what turned them on, how much pressure their balls could take, and whether or not they'd let her push a finger into their rear hole.

"Fuck me, baby. This is going to be over long before any of us want it to be if you don't stop sending out those visuals."

"If you two are done with the gab session, I'm looking forward to showing my mate how good we can make her feel."

Austin's growled words, centered Charlotte's mind, and for the next few minutes, she was able to lose herself in a level of pleasure she'd only read about. Everything faded but the electricity racing up and down her spine as Austin thrust in so deep, she felt him press against her cervix. Each time he shoved his cock between her swollen folds, Charlotte gasped around Israel.

"You are so fucking hot, baby. You are testing me in ways no woman ever has, Little Star."

Charlotte started seeing stars in her vision and wondered how much longer she could hold out against the onslaught of sensations. Her senses were overwhelmed as Austin increased the speed and force of his thrusts. Israel was fucking her mouth with shorter strokes that were every bit as devastating. Hearing a woman scream startled her until she realized it had been her voice bouncing off the walls, calling out Austin's name.

"*Mine.* You. Are. Mine, Charlotte."

She wasn't sure what sent her over—Austin calling her his or the final thrusts, so forceful, he scooted her up the bed. Israel tried to pull back, but she sucked him to the back of her throat until she felt hot spurts of his release. Swallowing the gift Israel had given her was hot as hell, but it was Austin who shattered her.

Feeling Austin's cock grow larger, pressing against the sensitized walls of her vagina a heartbeat before he shouted her name was all it took for her mind to splinter as lightning arced in every part of her body.

Feeling him jerk inside her as he buried his face against her neck, even in the fog of orgasm, Charlotte felt his teeth puncture her skin. A flood of warmth moved through her, and Charlotte wondered why she was floating above the bed. Austin's possessive growl and the erratic beating of her heart were the only sounds she could hear as she drifted several feet above the bed.

Watching the scene from above, Charlotte wondered for a few seconds if she'd died. Was it possible to die from pleasure overload? She didn't know, but it seemed reasonable, especially after what she'd just experienced. She knew the French referred to orgasm as *la petite mort*, literally, the little death, and who was she to argue?

"Come back to me, Charlotte. Baby, please."

The desperation in Austin's voice finally pulled her back, and when her eyes fluttered open, the relief in his eyes pulled at her heart.

"Fucking hell, I thought I'd lost you. Mating is supposed to be consensual, but I was so caught up in, well, in everything we shared." The calloused pads of his fingers smoothed over her cheek, luring her further under his spell. "Consent before mating is a Universal Law, Charlotte."

She'd been studying the Magical Laws her entire life, but she knew something Austin didn't. When Charlotte tried to speak, Austin shook his head, pressing his fingers against her lips. It was only then she realized she was tucked securely under the softest sheet she'd ever felt, and they'd managed to prop her up against pillows at the headboard. Looking to Israel, Charlotte was shocked to see the stricken look in his eyes as well.

"If you'd just—" Charlotte was cut off once again when Austin started to apologize again. Frustration filled her, and she'd finally had enough.

"I swear if you don't let me speak, I'm going to throw a world-class hissy fit." Both men gave her surprised looks before Austin finally motioned for her to continue. "I know the rules, Austin, but it doesn't matter… not really, because I'd have given my consent. I was just as lost in the moment as you were." Austin's shoulders sagged in relief before he pulled her against his chest, wrapping her tight in his arms.

"We'll still have to go before the Council. I have no idea what they'll say, but I'll accept whatever they deem appropriate."

Charlotte knew the members of the Council and wanted to put his mind at ease, but she doubted he'd listen to her. For now, all she could do was relish the security she felt listening to the steady beat of his heart beneath her ear.

Chapter Eight

"YOU CLAIMED CHARLOTTE the first time you fucked her?" Asia Adler stared at her brother's image on her phone and shook her head in amused disbelief. Hell, she'd never seen him this rattled.

"Don't be crass, Asia."

Holy crap, when did big brother get to be so prissy?

"When you were hiring an assistant, I gave you detailed reports on the top candidates. Did you read it?" Asia didn't try to hide the derision in her voice. She'd bet her brother had only read her summaries but wasn't sure he would admit it.

"I read enough. Besides, you always rank things in order of preference by stacking the best on the top, so I followed your lead. I'm glad I did, but why are you asking if I read the report?"

"You only read the damned synopsis, didn't you? I warned you about that, big brother. Why doesn't anybody ever listen to me? Cripes, I might as well talk to the damned wind." Asia was pissed. She compiled reports for Austin all the time, and he was making choices based on how things were stacked on his desk? What the hell was he thinking?

"And you made a choice simply because Charlotte's file was on top? Boy, oh boy. Maybe I'll get you a damned spinner, and you can use that to make decisions. I'll get one that's color-coded, so you don't have to read anything. Red for no, green for yes, and yellow for maybe."

"Damn, Asia, just tell me what was in the report I should have seen. You can read me the riot act later. Charlotte's spa treatments aren't going to last forever."

"And let me guess, you want to supervise because you don't want anyone touching your mate. Hell, I'm surprised you let her out of bed." His expression darkened, and for the first time in years, Asia wondered if she'd pushed her only older sibling too far.

"Okay, okay. No need to get pissy. Your mate is a magical, something I know you have already figured out. She is also a *very well connected* magical."

"What are you talking about?"

"She means my grandfather, aunt, and mother are on the Magical Council."

Austin spun around so fast, Asia was dizzy just watching the movement on her phone's small screen. "Damn it, Austin, set your phone down if you're going to practice your pirouettes."

"I'll talk to you later, little sister. And just so we're clear, you're still a pain in my ass."

Asia burst out laughing as her phone went dark. She should feel guilty for annoying her brother, but she didn't—some habits die hard, and pushing a sibling's buttons was always going to be entertaining. Shaking her head, Asia was still shocked Austin had claimed Charlotte without crossing all his t's and dotting all his i's. It was entirely out of character for him, and she wondered how much of this situation he'd share with the rest of the family when they all met in a few days for London's wedding.

Firing off a quick email to the resort where they were staying, Asia upgraded her brother's suite to a larger private villa nestled at the end closest to the beach. If he wasn't ready to share the news with everyone, it would be easier to convince the masses he brought his assistant along so they could work during their off hours if they were staying in a suite with more than two bedrooms since she was certain Israel was acting as their third. Forwarding a copy of the confirmation to both brothers, Asia hoped the gesture would make up for her earlier teasing.

Scrolling through her messages, Asia felt her heart skip a beat when she saw an email from Franklin Cordessi.

My Dearest Cara:

I'd be honored to accompany you to your sister's wedding celebration. I've cleared my calendar for several days both before and after the day of the wedding. Perhaps we can enjoy the extra time together. I am out of the country but plan to return to Houston tomorrow. I will stop by your office so we can finalize our plans and have dinner.

Yours,

Franklin

Asia felt a smile spread over her face as she opened her calendar and started making notes for her assistant. She quickly cleared a few extra days to spend with Franklin—since she hadn't had a vacation since before she joined

Adler Oil, Asia felt the break was long overdue.

"ARE YOU FUCKING kidding me? You had this information in your hands and didn't read it? Hell, no wonder Asia is pissed. She really doesn't get enough credit for everything she does for the company."

Although Austin agreed with Israel's comment about Asia's dedication to Adler Oil, he didn't appreciate the verbal slap-down. Several of his siblings, including Israel, had been encouraging him to delegate more. He had considered promoting a couple of his lower-level executives to executive vice-president, and now that he'd mated with Charlotte, the idea held even more appeal. For the last several years, Austin's life had centered around the business—it was time to reap some of the rewards for his dedication.

"You're right, Asia is amazing, and I'm not shifting any of this onto her shoulders." Although Charlotte's connection to the Magical Council was information that should have been included in her executive summary. Austin wondered why it hadn't been—even though he suspected his matchmaking sister had omitted the information on purpose.

"If you want to know about my connections to the Council, you just need to ask. I won't ever lie to you. And perhaps Asia didn't consider those contacts a negative."

Austin had been surprised to find Charlotte standing behind him. He knew she hadn't been standing there long because her scent immediately wrapped itself around him and before long, he'd be able to track her anywhere by her unique scent alone. He held out his hand and felt his heart swell when she didn't hesitate to cross the room to stand in front of him.

"Tell me who I'm going to be answering to, Little Star." If Charlotte had family members on the Council, it was going to make being called on the carpet damned interesting. She looked up at him and shook her head before grinning.

"You are worrying too much, Austin. They are going to listen to what I have to say. My mom is on the Council, her name is Amaya Sumner."

"Sumner?" Austin hadn't met Amaya or her husband, Eamon, but he'd heard of them. Amaya was said to have the power to control water/rain and wind while her husband was a summoner.

"I have always used my grandmother's maiden name. My parents knew most people with even a casual association with the magical community would recognize *Sumner*." She shrugged, but the nonchalant gesture didn't fool him.

Her emotions washed over him, and Austin frowned when he realized how excluded she'd felt in her own family. His family wasn't perfect, but they'd always had each other's backs. Hell, he couldn't imagine being forced to use another name.

"Anyone else?"

Israel was making breakfast and Austin appreciated his brother's attempt to speed the conversation along. The ladies from the spa would be arriving in a few minutes, and Austin would like to know what he was up against before they whisked Charlotte out to the rooftop terrace for a few hours of pampering.

"My mom's younger sister, Brigitte. I love my Aunt Gigi. She has always been my champion. She's fun and fiercely loyal."

"And a very powerful witch," Austin finished Charlotte's thought and smiled. He wondered if Charlotte knew her aunt was also a Domme.

"Yes, she is. Have you met her?"

Austin heard the insecurity in Charlotte's voice. She would soon learn, he was also fiercely loyal. He would never give her any reason to doubt his fidelity.

"I have, but only briefly." He'd let Brigitte tell her they'd met several years ago when they'd both helped with a training class for new members at Dark Desires.

"The Council is currently made up of five members, and apparently, you are related to two of them. Anyone else?" The truth was, Austin hated to ask. At different times during history, the Magical Council had varying numbers of members, but for the last decade, they'd functioned very efficiently with five members. Thinking she might be closely related to more than two members of the governing body of the entire magical community was daunting.

You should have read the fucking report.

Austin gave his brother a scathing glare over his shoulder, but Israel didn't seem to be intimidated. Turning his attention back to Charlotte, he watched as she looked everywhere but directly at him.

"Charlotte? I asked you a question." Austin cursed under his breath when he suddenly remembered Brigitte's last name. "Fuck me. Audric Stafford is your grandfather? The man whose first name literally means *old ruler*?" Israel whistled behind him as Austin shook his head and chuckled. Just fucking great, he'd mated the granddaughter of the most politically powerful wizard in the world without her prior permission.

"For what it's worth, my grandfather is one of the most open-minded people I know. If you haven't met him, I think you'll be pleasantly surprised."

Before Austin could reply, his phone vibrated in his pocket. Nodding to Israel when he checked the screen, Austin pulled Charlotte close for a quick hug.

"The spa staff is on their way up. Everything is already set up on the patio. Enjoy yourself, Little Star. My brother and I have big plans for you for the rest of the weekend."

They'd address her moving in with him after she was nicely relaxed. He'd already sent a crew to her apartment to pack her belongings. The men reported they'd been able to get everything in one trip, making Austin wonder how small her living space had been. It didn't make sense the granddaughter of the head of the Council of Magic was living like a damned pauper.

CHARLOTTE SMILED AT the two estheticians when they turned to her. She'd wondered if Austin and Israel were going to stay, they'd lingered so long. They'd assured her they would be checking in, and she didn't doubt for a moment they would. Sighing, she was grateful neither of the women seemed to find the Adler brothers behavior unusual.

"Don't worry, we're used to Doms watching over our shoulders. It will bother you more than it will us." Betsy, the older of the two women shrugged as she offered Charlotte a robe. "This will be yours to keep. Bring it with you the next time you visit Prairie Winds or Dark Desires, and we'll give you a discount and your own locker." Charlotte must have looked surprised because Betsy laughed. "Remember, we were trained by Tobi and Gracie. We'll take excellent care of you."

The younger woman, who'd introduced herself as Sarah, handed Charlotte a drink from the cooler they'd brought along. "Here, drink this. It's a mimosa... sort of. It has a bit more kick and will get you relaxed before your waxing."

Charlotte took a drink and hoped her eyes hadn't crossed as she felt herself shudder.

"Holy shit. What's in there?"

"It's Tobi's secret recipe. You'll have to find out from her because we don't even know. We get the concentrate already mixed and just add the orange juice. It's potent, isn't it?" Sarah laughed as she looked around the outdoor space. "This place is amazing. The landscape designer thought of everything." Pointing to a door marked as a changing room, she motioned Charlotte to follow her. "Let's get you changed while the wax reheats."

Fifteen minutes later, Charlotte was lying on a padded table with her legs spread wide open, every feminine secret exposed to Sarah's and Betsy's gazes. She'd been ready to bolt until she'd looked up into Austin's heated gaze. His dark eyes were focused on her face rather than her pussy, and his presence calmed her in a way she hadn't expected.

Moving to stand beside the table, he leaned down. When he spoke, his warm breath brushed the shell of her ear, making Charlotte shiver.

"You are going to love how much more sensitive you are after waxing. After we get back from the Caribbean, I'll set up laser treatments for you. After a few sessions, you'll be smooth forever." She felt a rush of moisture coat her sex and her cheeks heated with embarrassment. "Knowing your body responds to me is so fucking hot. Hell, just thinking about running my tongue along all those newly denuded folds has my cock about ready to burst."

Sarah yanked the first strip from her inner thigh, and Charlotte screamed into Austin's kiss. She wasn't sure how he'd known, but she was grateful he'd saved her the humiliation of shouting loud enough to be heard all over downtown Austin.

"Remember, you are doing this to please your Dom. I want you bare from the waist down. When I command you to present yourself to me later tonight, there won't be anything blocking my view. I can't fucking wait for dinner." With those parting words, he pressed a kiss against the tip of her nose, then walked away. *Walk away now, or you're going to end up fucking her. I shouldn't have assured Kent his staff would be back before the shops open later this afternoon. What the hell was I thinking, making that ridiculous promise?*

Austin's thought wafted through her mind, making Charlotte wonder if she should confess she'd started hearing him right after he'd claimed her. Another strip of wax was pulled mercilessly from her body, stealing all reasonable thoughts.

"Holy hell. Do you have any more of those drinks?

Maybe I should cut my stomach out of the deal and just mainline it? How much of it did you bring?" The women laughed as Betsy flipped open the lid of the cooler pulling out a large plastic pitcher. This time she poured the pain-numbing drink into a sports bottle.

"This will make it easier to drink lying down, and believe me, we brought enough to make your head feel like it's going to explode tomorrow morning. One of the many lessons Tobi and Gracie taught us was newbie subs are already suffering from sensory overload, they don't need us adding to the problem, so we'll numb your brain instead. We're here to help you make your Dom happy."

Betsy sounded as though she was speaking from experience, but Charlotte didn't get a chance to ask if she was also a member of Prairie Winds before another strip was pulled from the crease between her ass cheek and upper thigh.

"If these strips hurt this much, I'm glad you aren't waxing my who-ha." Both women went stock still, and Charlotte groaned. "He didn't order *that*, did he?"

"If by that, you mean a full Brazilian wax—then yes, he did. Didn't you hear me say I want you bare from the waist down?" Austin's voice sounded from the other side of the terrace, but Charlotte didn't think it would be a good idea to raise her head. The last time she'd tried to look around, the world spun clockwise.

"He's a demon. I don't think I've had enough to drink if you're going to smear wax between my ass cheeks and yank the hair out by the roots."

"On the contrary, sweetness. I think you've had more than enough to drink." Charlotte opened her eyes to see

Israel swimming in her view.

"Hold still, for heaven's sake." For the life of her, Charlotte couldn't figure out why Israel thought it was a good idea to weave back and forth above her. Hell, he was going to make her sick if he didn't stop that nonsense.

ISRAEL STOOD TO the side, partially hidden beneath the shaded palms, listening to the women banter. It gave him a unique glimpse at a side of Charlotte he hadn't previously seen. He'd learned a long time ago if you really wanted to understand a woman, you watched her interactions with her sisters or friends. After he'd finally stepped forward with the crackers and cheese he hoped would stem the alcohol's effects, Israel shook his head when she asked him to stand still.

"How many of Tobi's Mimosa bombs did she have?"

"She just started on her second, or maybe it's her third. I'm not really sure." Betsy and Sarah both shrugged, but he saw the concerned looks passing between them.

Israel appreciated Sarah trying to protect her client, and he almost smiled at her sudden focus on smearing warm wax over Charlotte's most intimate flesh.

Charlotte's lack of response to having a virtual stranger painting her pussy with hot wax was a testament to how inebriated the sweet sub was. She was definitely a lightweight when it came to alcohol—something they'd need to remember when they attended London's wedding. By the time Charlotte finished eating the snack he'd brought her, her pussy and ass were silky smooth. With the difficult part behind her, she'd be able to enjoy the extended massage they'd ordered.

"Call me when you are midway through her massage." Israel would give the ladies a short break while he pushed an inflatable plug into Charlotte's rosette. They would steadily inflate the remote-controlled plug during dinner, so she'd be ready to take them together later in the play-room. Both women grinned knowingly at him, nodding their understanding.

Israel stepped back inside just as a stunning redhead, dressed in a black leather bodysuit so tight, it looked like it had been painted on, emerged from a smoky mist. Glanc-ing to his right, Israel chuckled at the shocked look on Austin's face. Israel had never met the beauty, but the family resemblance was unmistakable.

"Damn, brother, you didn't tell me you were expecting a guest." Israel's comment and the woman's hearty laughter seemed to snap Austin out of his shocked stupor.

"Had I known Mistress B was going to arrive, I'd have let you know, but it seems Charlotte's Aunt Gigi wanted to make a surprise entrance."

Israel had to hand it to his brother, he'd packed a lot of valuable information into one sentence. Any witch power-ful enough to hold a seat on the Council of Magic would likely be capable of monitoring telepathic communication, so Israel kept his questions about *Aunt Gigi* to himself. The tension in the room was ratcheting up with each second, and Israel considered stepping back outside to see if there were any of Tobi's killer mimosas left.

Chapter Nine

AUSTIN WONDERED WHAT surprised him more—Brigitte's sudden appearance in his living room or the fact she'd chosen to show up in full Domme mode. It didn't say much for his observation skills he hadn't noticed how much Charlotte looked like Brigitte. If he'd ever seen them together, it would have been blatantly obvious the two women were related. He guessed the aunt and niece were nearly the same age, which meant they were probably closer than most.

"Brigitte, nice to see you again. Did you draw the short straw, or are you simply the advance team?" He knew full well he'd have to answer to more than one member of the Council. Claiming the granddaughter of the head of the Council on Magic without her prior consent wasn't going to be overlooked by anyone, but the longer he could delay the inevitable, the better. The better established his relationship was with Charlotte, the easier it would be to assure the five members of the magical communities' governing board he hadn't intended any harm or taken advantage of his lovely mate. He didn't want a shadow hanging over his claiming Charlotte.

"At least you didn't ask me why I'm here." Her voice

held a hint of teasing which he hoped meant the Council wasn't as upset as he'd feared. "I wanted to talk to you before Charley finishes with her spa treatments." Austin wasn't going to ask how she'd known what Charlotte was doing. With nine younger siblings, he'd learned a long time ago not to ask questions unless he was prepared to hear an answer he didn't like.

"For what it's worth, I wasn't surprised to learn my niece was at Prairie Winds, I suspected she was a submissive. I also know her father has been pressuring her to secure your help." He'd already heard Charlotte reference needing his help, but this might be an opportunity to get more information.

"What sort of help?" He stood with his feet shoulder-width apart, his arms crossed over his chest in a pose he knew she would recognize. The smile she gave him said she didn't intend to be a lot of help.

"Her father is the leader of a group of magicals who live in Cedar Bayou." She paused, giving the name time to register—it was a courtesy he hadn't needed. What would have helped was knowing why everyone seemed to think it was important to him.

"Did you ever watch Rudolph, the Red-Nosed Reindeer as a kid, Austin?" Her question surprised him, but without waiting for him to respond, Brigitte forged ahead. "Remember the Island of the Misfit Toys? That is how this group sees itself... they are a rag-tag assortment of various types and don't feel they have anywhere else to go." When he raised a skeptical brow, she shrugged. "I assure you, I've over-simplified the story, but it'll give you a frame of reference when Charley finds the courage to ask for your help."

"Why has she waited?"

"Charlotte wanted to have all the facts ready before she approached you, but her dad has been pushing her. She wanted to know all the details of the options you were considering, so she knew how to counter them."

Charlotte was easily one of the most efficient employees Adler Oil had ever hired, so it wasn't difficult to imagine her wanting to have everything in place before pleading her case. Frowning to himself, Austin wondered if her presence at Prairie Winds hadn't been as coincidental as he'd believed.

"I know that look, and you can wipe any questions you have about Charlotte's interest in the lifestyle being sincere right out of that skeptical mind of yours. The girl has been reading erotic romance novels for years, her interest in Dominance and submission isn't something she dreamed up to catch your eye. She has too much integrity for that sort of deception. Someday soon, I suggest you ask her why she's willing to work as your administrative assistant when she is a stone's throw from finishing her doctorate in economics."

Israel choked on the coffee he was drinking, and Austin shook his head.

"Damn it, that should have been in Asia's Executive Summary. I swear I'm going to offer Franklin big bucks to paddle her ass."

"Franklin Cordesi?" When Austin nodded, Brigitte sighed. "I tried to convince him to let me top him. He's deliciously dangerous." Austin shook his head because he doubted there was a chance in hell Cordesi was a switch.

"I hope there isn't a spell to turn a Dom into a submissive." Israel shuddered as he stepped forward extending his hand. "I'm Israel Adler, Ms. Stafford, it's nice to meet you." Austin watched as Israel charmed Brigitte, knowing they were each playing the other was almost amusing. *Almost.*

Austin stood back, listening to his brother casually inquire about the other members of the Council and was surprised to learn it didn't sound as if he'd be seeing any of the others anytime soon. Brigitte turned to him, her focus finally seemed to be on the elephant in the room no one was acknowledging.

"I want to speak to my niece before I leave town, but I don't want to interrupt her massage. Goddess knows, she's earned the pampering. I'm just here to make sure Austin understands his responsibility where my niece is concerned. Her family wants to ensure she is safe and happy... those are our chief concerns." Austin strongly suspected Charlotte's beloved Aunt Gigi was more interested in her happiness. If safety were the real issue, she'd have simply whisked her away.

"Charlotte's heart is safe with me. She is my mate—her safety and well-being will always be my number one priority, but that doesn't mean there won't be challenges. Even though she's been working for me, it will take us a while to get to know each other on a personal level."

"Not sure it can get much more personal, Austin." He heard equal parts snark and humor in Brigitte's tone but pushed aside his frustration. "Claiming without permission is usually a major issue, but I know Charlotte better than any of the other members of the Council. If Charlotte were unhappy, I'd have been the first person she called."

The sound of Israel's phone pinging drew Austin's attention. Knowing what his brother was planning, Austin gave an almost imperceptible nod toward the door.

Brigitte ambled slowly around the room, but her aimless wandering didn't fool him. Her father might be the head of the Magical Council, but this was a woman who had earned her seat on the well-respected governing body. Every member of the Council brought a unique skill set to the group, and Brigitte was no exception.

"Reading the energy of the room, Brigitte?" Engaging her in conversation was a mistake—anything that kept him from watching his brother shove a vibrating plug into Charlotte's sweet ass went in the mistake column—but he'd wanted Mistress B to know he was on to her. "Let me tell you what you're going to find. The only women who have been in this space for longer than a business get together are my sisters." Shrugging his shoulders, he couldn't hold back his grin. "Hell, even my playroom hadn't had a woman inside until last night."

"Ordinarily, I'd look forward to seeing it, but all things considered, I think I'll pass."

Austin chuckled because he understood her reluctance. He had no desire to *ever* see any of the playrooms his sisters played in—there were some things you didn't want to imagine when it came to family.

"Why don't you just paint red and white stripes on the damned thing? It should be mounted outside a barber shop. It's not going to fit up there!" Charlotte's shrieking voice preceded her.

Watching her storm through the door, wrapped in a thin white robe sent a bolt of heat surging through his blood. His wolf clamored for release and holding back those primal urges was testing him in ways he'd never imagined possible. The only thing that kept him from throwing her over his shoulder and stomping down the hall to the playroom was her shriek of joy when she saw Brigitte.

"Aunt Gigi."

Running into her beloved aunt's arms, Austin sensed the moment Charlotte realized what she'd been saying as she entered the living room. He felt her embarrassment but was impressed with the way she glossed over the awkwardness. Straightening her spine and stepping back, Charlotte's expression turned somber.

"If you're here to berate Austin, don't. I'm happy to be his mate and would have gladly given myself to him." Austin was thrilled to hear her reiterate what she'd said in the moments after he'd claimed her.

"Ladies, we'll leave you to chat for a few minutes." Zeroing in on Charlotte, Austin hoped his eyes conveyed how much he appreciated her words and how quickly he wanted to get her beneath him.

"Don't keep Israel waiting, Little Star. You've already racked up more punishment points than you can pay off in one session." The twinkle in her eyes told him she'd taken his words as a challenge. *Perfect.*

BRIGITTE TURNED TO her niece and grinned. "I told you he was hot."

"Well, hot doesn't quite cover it." Charlotte's pink

flush told Brigitte far more than her simple response.

"Oh, did I fail to mention he's a Dom? Oops, my bad." Gigi wasn't the least bit sorry and wouldn't claim she was.

"And you show up here looking like Debbie Domina-trix Does Dallas." Brigitte and Charlotte burst out in hysterical giggles, collapsing on a nearby sofa. "Goddess, I've missed you."

"Ditto, Charley. I swear, agreeing to that appointment on the Magical Council was the dumbest thing I've ever done. All work and no play makes Gigi a dull and very cranky Mistress." Charlotte chuckled, shaking her head.

"How did I not know? I can't believe I was so naïve."

"Humbling, isn't it? Remember this moment. Someday you'll look back on it as a life lesson meant to teach you to look past the veneer people present to the public. We all have chapters in our life stories we don't read aloud." Charlotte made a gesture meant to imitate gagging, making Gigi laugh. "If we were in a club, that bratty behavior would get you turned over to a Dom for punish-ment although that's probably not going to happen now. Austin only shares with his brother, and that will change soon enough."

"How long until my mother shows up? Or is she busy with some life or death matter on the other side of the planet?"

Brigitte heard the echo of a lifetime of disappointments in her niece's voice and felt her heart clench, knowing how often Amaya had let her only child down. Hell, both Charley's parents had been far too involved in their own lives to be bothered with their daughter until they'd discovered how gifted she was. Even then, their interests had been self-serving. To those outside their inner circle, it looked like Amaya and Eamon had been devoted to protecting their young daughter—they had but not for the reason everyone assumed.

"She'll check in, but I doubt it's anytime soon. She is in BFE, working on some secret project." Gigi knew her sister would make an appearance more to maintain an appearance of the concerned mother than to make certain her daughter wasn't trapped in a situation where her skills would be compromised. Right now, Amaya was indeed stuck in bum-fuck Egypt, working on a spell to keep the region as stable as possible.

"Keep your eyes open for your grandfather on your vacation, I expect he'll pop in when you least expect him. He'll want to check on you himself. You'll both be soaking up the sun while I toil away in whatever godforsaken hellhole they send me to next." Gigi snickered at the look on Charley's face. Obviously, the woman she'd always considered more of a friend than simply her niece wasn't buying a guilt trip ticket today.

"Oh, I'm only going along to work. I probably won't make it out of the hotel's business center." The thought of being stuck inside while Austin's family soaked up the warm sunshine was enough to make her earlier high spirits plummet. She loved the sound of the ocean beating against the sandy shore as palm trees waved in the breeze.

"Damn, I hate the thought of being stuck inside when I want to feel my toes sinking into the warm sand. Lying on a lounger where I can hear the upbeat sounds of Caribbean music, sipping on some fruity concoction sounds almost as appealing as the massage waiting for me outside."

Brigitte recognized the hint for what it was and stood, pulling Charley to her feet at the same time. "Places to go. Things to do." Gigi gave her niece a quick hug before turning her to face the door. "Go get your massage, you deserve it.

"Talk to Austin... tell him what's troubling you about Cedar Bayou. If you wait until you have all the facts, it'll be too late. Sometimes, you have to shoot from the hip." Giving the younger woman one last quick hug, Gigi stepped back and disappeared into a cloud of blue smoke.

"Aunt Gigi, you always did have a flair for the dramatic." The only sound Charley heard was her Aunt's hearty laughter sounding from a distance. Turning, Charlotte bounced off Austin's broad chest.

Chapter Ten

"DROP THE ROBE, Charlotte."

Austin's deep voice vibrated all the way to her core, pulling her back from the brief moment of panic she'd experienced when she'd run into him. After being locked in the cage as a kid, Charlotte had never fully recovered from the fear of having someone creep up on her.

"Holy shit, you scared ten years off my life. Don't sneak up on me like that." Austin raised a brow, pointedly looking down at the robe she was still wearing.

"You can take it off, or I can take it off for you, but my help will come at a price." His deep voice conveyed what was probably meant as a threat even though it sounded to her more like a promise than something she should worry about. Charlotte untied the robe's belt, and with tantalizing deliberation let the soft cotton fabric slide off her shoulders.

"You're exquisite, mate." Austin didn't move. Studying everything about her, he wanted to cheer when he saw goose bumps race up her arms. "Knowing you belong to me makes me want to claim you again and again." Tracing his fingers from her shoulder down to encircle her wrist, he marveled at how fragile she felt in his hold. With a deliberate show of patience, he turned her to face Israel.

"You know you're in trouble, don't you, sweetness? Storming away from a Dom your Master tasked with preparing you will always earn you a punishment. Since the ladies are waiting for you outside, we'll make this quick." Israel started to lead her to the back of the sofa, but Austin must have sensed her growing panic.

"What's your safe word, Little Star?"

"Red, Sir. Yellow if I need to slow down or ask a question." Charlotte wasn't sure what Israel had planned, but she found comfort knowing Austin wasn't abandoning her. She heard him growl deep in his throat before his hand wrapped around her upper arm halting her progress.

"I'll never abandon you, Charlotte. You are my mate, you will always be able to count on me having your back." He stroked the side of her face with a tender touch that took her by surprise before he stepped back. "Take this punishment with grace so you can enjoy the rest of your massage, then we'll play. I'm looking forward to showing you how much more sensitive your pussy is now, and my favorite kink store delivered a couple of pieces of specialty jewelry for you a few minutes ago."

Looking deep in Austin's eyes, Charlotte saw past the determined businessman she dealt with every day. The man standing in front of her was edgier, more intense. The wave of emotion she felt surrounding her was comforting and arousing at the same time. Knowing Austin felt possessive of her, that her safety and well-being were important to him settled something in her.

Ten minutes later, Charlotte struggled to find a comfortable position on the massage table. Shifting again for the third time in ten seconds, Betsy smiled knowingly down at her and Charlotte felt her cheeks flush.

"We'll give the arnica time to work its magic on your tender backside before attempting to massage that side."

"Israel didn't take my sass very well." She tried to keep the snark out of her tone but wasn't sure she'd succeeded when the other woman smiled.

"I've been in the lifestyle long enough to know it never pays to argue about a plug. Dom's get snarky about bratty behavior, but they get positively irate about plugs."

"Yep. You kick up a fuss, and they just find a bigger plug to shove up your bottom." Sarah's giggle from above her made Charlotte smile.

Knowing neither of the women were judging her based on her earlier outburst helped settle her roiling nerves. Their easy camaraderie was just what she needed after everything she'd been through the last twenty-four hours. *Face it, you've been wound up like an eight-day clock since you started working for Austin.*

AUSTIN STOOD IN the shadows, watching the interaction between his mate and the ladies from Prairie Winds. Charlotte was so new to the lifestyle, he'd worried she'd needed more aftercare, but Austin knew the women needed to get back to the club and didn't want to make them late. Pulling two large bills from his wallet, he folded each one individually, tucking them into his shirt pocket.

"That's a hefty tip, brother."

Israel's amused voice came from over his left shoulder,

making Austin wonder who his brother had been talking to on the phone. There were times Austin wished he could throw his damned phone under the nearest bus, and from the look Israel had given him, he had a similar sentiment. When Austin didn't respond, Israel nodded his head to the door. Stepping back inside, Austin headed for the bar. Whatever Israel had to say would evidently be easier to hear over a finger of Scotch—not a good sign.

"Cedar Bayou borders land Adler Oil purchased last year—and when I say borders, that's an understatement. The undeveloped land the company acquired surrounds the bayou on three sides with a narrow strip for access leading into the place where Charlotte was raised. Asia being Asia, inserted a clause in the purchase agreement that gives Adler Oil first right of refusal for a hundred years.

"I remember being surprised the seller was willing to leave that in the contract, but the name Cedar Bayou still doesn't ring a bell." It was unusual for Austin to forget details of a land acquisition—even one the company hadn't planned to develop immediately.

"It was only described with a metes and bounds description—it wasn't specifically named. I think the seller was worried you might be spooked if he told you who lived in the middle of his land purchase."

Austin nodded because the man he'd dealt with hadn't known Austin's own secret. Leaning back against the kitchen counter, his ankles crossed, Austin considered the implications of what he'd just learned.

"I don't know what the solution is, but I'm looking forward to hearing what my mate has to say." Shaking his head, he set the empty glass aside before crossing his arms over his chest. "Why would she hold back telling me? Hell, I'm not that scary." Israel shrugged his shoulders.

"There are plenty of people who would be happy to argue that particular point with you, but I think you already know that."

Austin chuckled because Israel was right. He'd been forced to build a reputation as a tough negotiator quickly after their parents were killed in a car crash he still wasn't convinced was an accident.

"You've said yourself, Charlotte is a detail person. Can you imagine her coming to you with a business proposal without having all her ducks in a row?"

Israel had a valid point. Charlotte was the most organized administrative assistant he'd ever had. She'd streamlined several of the functions he'd spent too much time dealing with. Hell, her efficiency had been the reason he'd gotten home in time to attend the club last night—the irony of the entire situation wasn't lost on him.

Tuning in to Charlotte, Austin felt her soft sighs of pleasure as her muscles relaxed under the manipulation of Betsy's skilled hands. His cock began to swell as he thought about what they had planned for her. Introducing her to the mysterious connection between pleasure and pain would be a privilege, but first, they had to get through dinner. He hoped their guests arrived early enough he'd have time to speak with Micah Drake and Jax McDonald before their meal.

When Micah called earlier today to say he'd uncovered something interesting related to Cedar Bayou, Austin hadn't been surprised since Micah's and Jax's positions at Prairie Winds gave them access to information from many restricted sources. Micah's sources were often military which added another layer of intrigue because Austin couldn't imagine what possible interest the U.S. military could have with a small tract of land in the middle of a land purchase he'd made recently.

An hour later, Austin stood in his home office, listening as Micah outlined what he'd learned. Hearing the military had been tracking Charlotte for years was unsettling. Their interest wasn't widely known, or Cameron Barnes would have been in the loop, particularly considering Cedar Bayou's proximity to Houston. Jax McDonald, Micah's long-time friend and partner in their polyamorous marriage with Gracie, spoke up, giving voice to Austin's confusion.

"I heard about your conversation with Cam last night at the club, and I find it damned odd he wasn't in the know on this. Even though it's domestic, it's still too close to home for him to have been left out."

"They probably thought he'd be biased since I've applied for membership in Master Cameron's club."

Charlotte's voice sounded from behind Austin, and he wanted to growl in frustration at having forgotten to lock the door. *Why the hell doesn't anyone stay where I put them?*

CAMERON BARNES READ the message from Micah Drake, seething with frustration by the time he'd finished the attached reports. It was one thing for Homeland Security to play in his backyard, it was another for them to do so without letting him know what they were up to. Pulling out his phone, he started to scroll through his contacts when he felt his wife's warm hands settle on the top of his shoulders.

"Take a deep breath, Master." Dr. Cecelia Barnes knew him better than anyone else in the world, and her ability to sense when he was near the edge never ceased to amaze him. "Your muscles are tied in knots. I think I could help you relieve some of that tension." He smiled over his shoulder at her. With her career as one of the leading pediatric surgeons in the world, their children, and his business interests, it was rare for them to have time alone.

"Do you now? What do you have in mind?" Before they became parents, Cam had insisted CeCe remained naked anytime she was in the penthouse suite they'd shared atop Dark Desires in Houston. There were days he longed for those simpler times.

"Whatever pleases you, Master." She practically purred her answer.

Fucking perfect. Everything about his woman called to him. For years, he'd sworn playing with subs was enough—until he met CeCe. She'd changed his life in an instant, but it took him years to realize it. Wrapping his hand around her right wrist, he gently pulled her around until she was standing between his knees.

"You please me in ways you can't imagine, pet—and you're right, I'm wound pretty tight. Carl is filling in at Dark Desires tonight. Are you sure you're ready for how this might play out? We haven't had an entire evening to ourselves for a long time, and you know how demanding I can be." Carl Phillips was the other member of their triad; he'd filled a role in their Dom/sub relationship Cam nor CeCe had known was missing. Studying her closely, he felt his heart swell with pride as the slow smile spreading over her face told him everything he needed to know.

"What's your safe word, love?" It didn't matter they'd been together for years. Safe, sane, and consensual was more than a tenet he followed at the club—it was fundamental to everything he believed in. Listening as she repeated the answer he'd heard so many times before settled something in Cam, putting him in a far better frame of mind. "I want you to bring two bottles of water with you to the playroom in five minutes, pet."

After she'd left his office, Cam sent off a quick text to Carl, then slid his phone in his pocket. He'd never taken the damned thing into the playroom, priding himself on maintaining a single-minded focus on his submissive, but tonight, he needed to know if the situation with Charlotte Hays changed. Having been kept in the dark made him distrustful of the agency poking around in his neck of the woods—as his grandfather used to say. DHS made a mistake poking around right next door, messing with a woman who hadn't even received her acceptance letter yet. Targeting one of the members of his club was another strike. But the final blow was learning about this from Micah Drake. Damn it all to hell, he hated not being the most informed person in his circle of friends. Shaking his head at the immature path his thoughts had taken, Cam made his way to his playroom.

"You take my breath away, pet." Naked and kneeling just inside the door, her knees were spread wide, giving him an unobstructed view of the glistening folds of her pussy. "Before we start, I want you to know Carl is not happy he's missing this." Squatting down in front of her, he trailed his fingers along the underside of her jaw. "He wanted me to tell you he will expect equal time." Lifting her face so he could meet her gaze, he saw love and desire reflected in her eyes. The intoxicating mixture called to him on multiple levels.

Taking her hand in his, Cam helped CeCe to her feet. Leading her to the large open frame across the room, he made quick work of securing her inside the custom made wooden structure. He listened as her breathing became shallower and watched the pulse-pounding at the base of her throat. No matter how often they played, she was always perfectly responsive. Knowing this brilliant woman put herself in his hands was humbling, the gift of her trust would always be his most treasured possession.

Trailing a length of silk over one shoulder, he let the tail of the scarlet fabric fall like water between her shoulder blades before it kissed the rounded globes of her ass. Lifting the sash back up and over the other shoulder, Cam positioned it over her eyes, tying it at the back of her head.

"Your trust is a gift, pet." He felt more than heard her sweet sigh of surrender. Picking up his favorite flogger, Cam let the fronds skim over the top swell of her ass, smiling at the shiver he saw move up her spine. Leaning forward to nip the top of her shoulder, Cam outlined the shell of her ear with his tongue.

"Shall we begin, love?" The first fall of the flogger had enough sting to make her hiss, so he repeated it on the other side. "I asked you a question, pet, and I expect an answer."

"Yes, Master, I'm ready whenever it pleases you." Her voice was already taking on the airy, disconnected tone he loved so much.

Pushing her into subspace was one of his greatest pleasures. Blanking his mind, pushing out all thoughts but those of everything but the woman bound before him, Cam set an inconsistent pace to keep her guessing—he found it was the key to delaying her release as long as possible. *Who are you kidding, Barnes? Those sexy gasps and sweet pleading are going to push you over the edge long before she gives in?* What the hell, they had all night—those damned phone calls he planned to make could wait until morning.

Chapter Eleven

AUSTIN HELD OUT his hand, and Charlotte didn't hesitate to move to his side. She'd known they would be discussing her, and despite Gracie's best efforts to keep her occupied, Charley wasn't going to let them make decisions without having all the facts. She certainly wasn't going to allow them to discuss her future without being included in the discussion. Mated or not, she was determined to maintain her independence.

"Talk to us, Charlotte."

Austin's simple words bolstered her confidence in more ways than he knew. Not only had he just made it clear her opinion was valued, he'd also reassured her she'd made the right decision allowing him to claim her. He might think he'd made the move all alone, but she could have stopped him and had chosen not to. In her mind, that made her just as responsible for their present situation.

Explaining the political makeup of the group her father governed wasn't easy because they were such an eclectic mix of magicals—each with their own customs and unique abilities. She'd spent years in the bayou and still didn't understand how her father managed to keep so many people with incredibly varied interests happy.

Over the years, her grandfather had popped in for occasional visits—she hadn't realized until much later they always followed her discovering a new skill. The best way she could describe her dad was he reminded her of an aging college professor stuck in the hippy mindset. He still wore Birkenstocks and faded blue jeans. His hair was too long, and he was fully committed to a *laissez-faire* lifestyle, despite his leadership position. Charlotte did her best to explain the workings of her family and the residents of Cedar Bayou but wasn't sure she'd succeeded.

"I'm close to finishing my education, and my father always hoped I'd return to take over for him. My thesis is on developing alternative economic strategies for the Gulf Coast. Unfortunately, the owners of the land surrounding Cedar Bayou decided to sell before I could present my proposals to them." *Picture a '60s hippy commune with witches, wizards, fairies, and sprites.*

"So, you were on track to finish your Ph.D. before quitting to work at Adler Oil?" She could hear the disgruntled tone in Austin's voice, but Charlotte was determined to stand her ground.

"Yes. It was important for me to gather all the information I could before approaching you. I didn't think you would take me seriously unless I'd crossed all the t's and dotted all the i's. I didn't want you to see me as some tree-hugger who was only trying to prevent you from utilizing an investment you'd spent millions acquiring."

The tension in the room was so thick, you could practically see it floating in the air. As a rule, she wasn't intimidated by tension. Charlotte had become immune to skeptics and bullies many years ago, but this time, there was too much at stake… and *this time*, it was *personal.*

———

AUSTIN HAD PLANNED to let Charlotte continue without interrupting her with his questions or comments, but when he felt her insecurity, he pulled her close.

"Everyone here is on your side, Charlotte. We are trying to figure this whole thing out, and we need all the information you can give us." Jax McDonald stepped forward and smiled down at her. At six foot eleven inches in height, the only thing that kept Jax from being intimidating as hell was his warm smile. "Before this goes any further, I have a favor to ask."

Looking at Micah, Austin saw the other man grinning and Gracie shaking her head.

"Honestly, you are worse than the kids, Master." Austin suspected Gracie's use of the honorific had saved her ass—literally. None of their reactions phased Jax, he kept his unwavering gaze on Charlotte.

"I want to see you disappear into a mist. I watched the club surveillance video, but…"

"Yeah, he watched it about a hundred times—until the rest of the security team wanted to pull their hair out." Micah rolled his eyes, and Gracie giggled, making Charlotte grin.

"Please? I've never known anyone who could do anything this cool." Austin shook his head and chuckled at the man's childlike curiosity. At six foot eleven, Jax McDonald was a hulking man—a former NFL player who'd never lost the bulk.

Austin stared at the man who didn't bat an eye when high-ranking military and political figures walked into Prairie Winds. Seeing Jax utterly captivated by his mate's skills was oddly satisfying.

Charlotte grinned, then vanished in the same silvery mist he'd seen across the room last night. He could still feel her pressed against his side but couldn't see her.

"Fucking awesome." Jax's enthusiastic response brought a chuckle from Micah and a frown from their beautiful wife.

"I'd get spanked for saying that." She looked to the spot where Charlotte had been a moment earlier and shrugged. "It's not fair, I tell you. We get paddled for profanity, and the Doms can use it to express joy. Where's the justice in that?"

He felt Charlotte giggle against him as she slowly came back into view.

"Hell, no wonder Uncle Sam wants you." Jax still didn't know the full extent of Charlotte's powers. Austin looked down at Charlotte as she slowly reappeared. He wasn't going to throw her under the bus, but he hoped she'd tell the others the rest of the story. She sighed and shook her head.

"They might be interested in shimmering, but that's probably not the top thing on their wish list."

"It's your ability to heal others, isn't it, Charlotte?" Jax looked stunned, but Micah smiled knowingly before shrugging. "There were mentions of it buried in the report, but the investigators couldn't find any solid evidence, just rumors." When she slowly nodded, it was Micah's turn to swear. "Holy shit. I'm not going to ask you to prove it because I believe you, but damn, that would definitely put you high on their recruitment list. Those two abilities would make you a hell of a teammate on a mission."

"What would happen if you were pregnant? Would the baby disappear, also?" Gracie's question shocked everyone in the room, including Charlotte.

"I don't know. To be honest, I've never thought about it. I'll ask my grandfather when I see him. Now you've piqued my curiosity as well."

"Why is Cedar Bayou so important?" Again, Gracie asked a question many of them hadn't focused on. This time Charlotte blushed.

"Ley lines. Three of them intersect at the center. The lines of energy combined with the power of three make it a sacred and powerful location for magicals. We've been lucky to fly under the radar for centuries, but a large-scale mineral exploration would disrupt the energy flow in a way no one could every repair. Their unique combined energy also means there are so unique plants growing there. Their healing properties are vastly underrated."

"Ley lines? Aren't those supposed to be underground paths of energy or something?" Austin was impressed with Gracie's basic knowledge of something most outside their kind paid any attention to.

"Yes, and I assure you, they are very real. There are even some magicals who can use them for travel." Charlotte's answer couldn't have been more accurate.

Austin glanced at Israel and saw him holding back a grin. They knew too well how a magical could tap into the power of the lines for travel—their brother Cleveland had been using them for years.

"Did the seller know all this, Charlotte?" Israel asked the question Austin had been ready to ask, proving he was tuned in as usual. Even though they weren't the closest in age, the two of them had always been exceptionally close.

"He wasn't magical, but he'd become friends with my dad... that's why he left the narrow passage access and the bayou itself out of the sale." Austin felt a wave of sadness move over her as if it had been his own emotion. "Al didn't want to sell the land, but his wife is ill, and he wanted to make certain she had the best care available." When he raised a brow in question, she shook her head. "It isn't anything I can help with, she has dementia. It's sad watching her mind slip away."

She's going to make a wonderful mother.

Nodding once, acknowledging Israel's comment, Austin was grateful for their silent connection. They had been communicating telepathically so long, it was easy to lock it down to just the two of them. He hated excluding his mate, but he didn't want to distract her. He was relieved she felt safe enough to speak openly with Micah, Jax, and Gracie.

Charlotte continued to answer Micah's and Jax's questions during dinner, but it was easy to see she was nearing an emotional edge. They set aside their plans to play during their meal, hoping she'd get a chance to visit with Gracie and unwind, but the sweet woman was just as inquisitive as her men.

It's time to move this to the playroom. I don't want this evening to end up being all about business.

Twenty minutes later, both subs were naked and secured to pieces of equipment in the playroom. Gracie was bent over the spanking bench, her golden tan thighs framing the glistening folds of her deep rose-colored sex. Jax and Micah were finally focused on their own woman instead of interrogating Charlotte. Austin was surprised at the relief he felt having his mate out of their spotlight. Watching their full attention center on Gracie was a testament to Jax and Micah's ability to center their attention on the woman who owned their hearts, despite their apparent interest in Charlotte's situation.

Gathering the toys he and Israel planned to use during their scene, Austin kept glancing at Charlotte—gauging her reactions as Israel secured her to the medical table at the far side of the room. The multi-functional straps and drop-down edges made this piece of equipment an ideal option for their scene. He'd paid a master craftsman an exorbitant amount of money to make the piece to his exact specifications, and ironically, it had been installed just last week. It didn't matter how many examples he saw, the perfect timing of the Universe always amazed him.

Wheeling the metal tray to the side of the table, Austin was glad he'd had the foresight to cover the tray since Ms. Inquisitive wasn't even trying to hide her interest. Lifting the silk scarf from the tray, he grinned at Israel. *Let's make sure our sweet sub is well prepared for what we have planned for later, brother.*

CATALINA ADLER STOOD in the hotel room's large marble bathroom, staring blankly at the battered woman staring back from the mirror. She had no idea how long she'd been standing there, but her nipples were drawn tight from the chill in the room, and goose bumps raced over the bruised surface of her skin.

"Jesus, Cat, what are you doing?" Moving her gaze to the man stepping through the door, Catalina saw worry etched in his expression. "Come on, Princess, let's get you warmed up." He pulled a robe from a nearby hook, wrapping it around her before picking up a wide-tooth comb from the counter. Leading her into the bedroom, he settled her on the bed before moving behind her. "Sit still while I comb your hair, then I want you to eat something before you sleep."

Catalina still couldn't believe Cooper Hicks had found her... she'd been convinced she was going to die in that small cement room. The men who'd kidnapped her had been methodical in their beatings, they hadn't touched her face, insisting the CIA wouldn't give them what they wanted if they couldn't recognize her. They may have left her face alone, but her torso was so bruised, she could barely pull in enough air to speak.

"Fucking hell, Catalina, don't cry. I can't even hug you because of the way your body has been battered. My only regret is I can't kill the bastards again."

"Thank you. I don't know if I told you how relieved I was to see you walk through that door. I don't know how you did it, but you saved my life." Cat didn't want to cry because sucking in a deep breath was excruciating. Cooper had already assured her he hadn't given her siblings any information about her injuries, but insisted she needed to talk to them at London's wedding in a couple of days.

"You're welcome, Princess." The nickname used to

annoy her, but this time Catalina felt the affection attached to it.

She could feel him braiding her hair and sighed when she realized he hadn't said anything about her hair color. *Damn, he must really be worried if he isn't teasing me.*

"What was that sigh for, Cat?"

"I just noticed you haven't commented on my hair, so obviously I'm a serious train wreck if you don't think I can take it." She felt him chuckle behind her as he pulled her back against his chest and gently wrapped his arms around her. "I thought I was hallucinating when you came through that damned iron door, then I heard you whisper my name, and it was all I could do to not burst into tears." The truth was, she'd never been so happy to see anyone in her entire life.

COOPER PULLED CATALINA closer as gently as he could until she was resting against his chest, trying to get his emotions under control before she sensed how truly terrified he'd been when he'd learned she'd been kidnapped. From the little bit she'd said, he knew she had no idea how long she'd been locked in that fucking concrete cell.

What few favors he hadn't called in during his search for her were being used now to keep her family from finding out what she'd been through and descend on her like a pack of wolves. Rolling his eyes at the irony, Cooper took a deep breath and sent up a silent prayer of thanks for the opportunity to hold her in his arms. A knock at the door broke the spell.

"That'll be your soup, Princess. Come." Helping her to her feet, Cooper led Catalina to the suite's large open area. Her steps faltered when she saw the men standing around the table, but she recovered quickly. Smiling, Cat started to extend her arm to shake hands and groaned. Sam McCall shook his head as the petite whirlwind wife he shared with his brother, Sage, darted around them.

"Stop." Cooper's sharp command barely fazed Jen, but she came to an immediate halt in front of Catalina when Sage repeated the command. The little blonde pixie gave Cooper a scathing look, making him shake his head and grin as he watched Sam pull open the door. The young men wheeling in their room service order looked at Sam with something between suspicion and awe. At six foot three, Sam was considerably taller than the average adult male in this part of the world, but it was his linebacker build that intimidated most people.

"Sweet cheeks, you are going to pay for that look. Someday, Cooper will call in that chip."

Cooper chuckled at Sage's teasing tone. It hadn't taken long to figure out Sage wasn't as strict, but he was every bit as dominant as his brother. It was interesting to watch them tag team the woman they shared—it seemed they each brought something to the relationship that Jen needed.

"Oh, everybody is always threatening retribution until Master Sage is busy kicking ass... ets, and I'm needed to fly people out. Boy, oh boy, then Jen is a hot commodity, and all those trivial offenses don't seem so important anymore. No, siree. Jen's everybody's best buddy and pal." Sage was shaking his head and chuckling at her nonsense. There was something about Jen's fiery spirit that reminded Cooper of his sister, Lakyn. Jen gave Catalina a hug so gentle, even as battered as she was, he wondered if she'd felt it.

"It's nice to see you again, Cat. I wish it were under better circumstances." Leaning closer, she whispered, "I'm glad those piss-titted wienies didn't know who you really work for." Cooper couldn't have agreed more—had the kidnappers known Catalina was anything other than a world-renowned jewelry designer who catered to her mega-wealthy clients by jetting all over the world, they'd have beaten her to within an inch of death.

As soon as the small group of rescuers got some rest, they'd be on their way to the airport. Cooper knew he wouldn't be able to let down his guard enough to fall asleep until they were in the air. The medication the military doctor had given him for Catalina would help her rest comfortably on the long flight. The McCalls would make a stop in the Caribbean before heading home to Texas. Cooper had already arranged for their clothing for London's wedding to be waiting at the resort. *Maybe a few days on the beach will help my heart rate return to normal and my adrenaline level to level out.*

Who was he kidding? He'd lost at least a decade from his life between the phone call telling him she'd been pulled off the street and the overwhelming relief he'd felt when he'd opened the door to find her terrified, but alive. Refocusing his attention on the verbal sparring taking place around him, Cooper kept a careful watch on Catalina.

He doubted the men who'd held her captive had bothered to provide anything other than a few stale pieces of bread for her to eat, so he needed to be sure she had something substantial in her belly before she fell asleep and dropped like a stone—and the crash was coming... quickly. His one comfort was knowing the group wouldn't be kidnapping anyone else—Sam had taken one look at the carnage and grumbled about Cooper not leaving any of the fun for him. *You have to love former SEALs, they are always up for a good time and their idea of fun always involved carnage.*

Cooper might not have been on the McCall's team, but they had worked together on occasion. Knowing he'd be working with former Special Forces members had been one of the deciding factors in his decision to join the Prairie Winds team.

Now, I just need to convince Catalina to do the same.

Chapter Twelve

C HARLOTTE FELT LIKE she was floating down the hall of Austin's penthouse. Searching her mind, she tried to find something that made sense among the remnants of memories drifting aimlessly in her head. The last thing Charlotte remembered was feeling like her entire body was going to burst into flames. When it finally registered she was in Austin's arms, she was finally able to lift her heavy lids when he laid her on the bed.

"Welcome back, Little Star." *Welcome back? Where did I go?* "Watching you soar into subspace was so hot." It took her a few seconds to remember he could hear her thoughts. At least that explained why he'd answered her unspoken questions. It was a relief to know Austin and Israel hadn't melted her brain.

Austin covered her body with his own, his lips sealing over hers in a blistering kiss that stole her breath and sent lightning down her spine before the buzz settled once again in her sex. When she sighed, he took advantage and pushed his tongue forward, exploring every recess of her mouth. She'd already experienced what his talented tongue could do to her nipples, and how close to the edge of sanity that skill could push her as it swept through the folds of her sex, but the intimacy of his kiss pushed everything else to the back of her mind.

Every time Austin touched her, Charlotte could feel their bond strengthen. She'd read a lot about shifters and mating, but nothing she'd read had prepared her for the all-consuming connection and soul-deep yearning to have him inside her as often as possible. The books she'd read insisted the sexual drive would lessen after a few weeks, but she wasn't sure she wanted it to.

"Need is vibrating from the deepest recesses of your very soul, Charlotte. Israel and I aren't finished with you yet, baby." Lifting her as if she weighed nothing at all, Austin turned her to where Israel was already settled on the bed, stroking his latex covered cock.

"Come here, sweetness. Straddle me and take me into your tight pussy." Israel's voice was gravel rough, making her wonder how close he was to losing control.

She moved the tip of his latex covered cock through her wet folds before sinking down, taking his entire length inside her. Israel moaned beneath her, reassuring Charlotte she wasn't the only one affected by the fire he ignited in her core.

"Fuck me, sweetness, your vaginal walls are already quivering around me. Your Master better hurry, or he's going to miss the party."

THERE WASN'T A chance in hell Austin was going to miss this party. They'd stretched Charlotte's tight rear hole with the plug, inflating it several times while she'd been on the medical table in the playroom. Using a generous squirt of lube, he massaged the tight ring of muscles surrounding her ass, grateful how quickly they loosened.

Pull her against your chest and hold on. I don't want her bucking back against me and tearing the delicate tissues before they're adequately stretched.

"Come here, sweetness. Let me hold you close while Austin stretches out your sweet ass. We're going to send you over the moon, sweetness."

Austin watched Charlotte's body relax against his brother and was grateful for Israel's soothing tone. Slipping two fingers inside her back entrance, Austin scissored his digits several times before pulling them free, then leaned down to nip her shoulder.

"Let's do this right this time, Little Star. Do you want to belong to me?" Austin felt his incisors begin to lengthen as he started pressing his cock against her rosette.

"Yes. Please. I need…"

"I know what you need, love."

Austin was practically panting, his own need demanding action long before he finally pushed the head of his cock past the tight ring of muscles of Charlotte's ass. The heat of her body was searing him in ways he'd never believed possible. Nodding to Israel, Austin pushed deep at the same time his brother lifted Charlotte so only the head of his cock remained inside her slick channel.

Setting a fast pace, the men made certain one of them was deep inside her hot body at all times, alternating perfectly timed strokes until they felt her shatter between them. The strength of her orgasm shocked Austin, barely giving him time to sink his teeth deep into the sensitive place where her shoulder joined her neck.

Once again, he felt fire racing through his entire body as they exchanged DNA. He wondered briefly what skills they would give to one another, but the question was fleeting as pure pleasure flooded every cell in his body. Austin found himself lost in a vortex of swirling colors, wondering if he was being sucked into an alternate plane of existence.

Thank the Great Goddess his instincts took over while his mind was touring outer space because he was licking the puncture wounds on her neck when he finally came back to earth. The holes closed quickly, leaving small scars over the top of those barely visible from the night before. Pulling himself from the tight grasp of her ass, Austin immediately felt the loss of their connection. Israel looked like he'd been run over by a truck, and it was all Austin could do to keep from laughing.

"Come on, Little Star, you've leveled Israel. Hell, from the look on his face, I'm not sure he'll ever be the same. Let's take a quick shower, then get some rest."

Charlotte didn't know it yet, but they were leaving tomorrow morning for the Caribbean. He wanted to spend time celebrating their mating, and what better place than a sandy beach? By the time they returned from the wedding celebration, the moving crew he'd hired would have moved all Charlotte's belongings into the penthouse. They'd been instructed to bring everything from her parent's house as well as what little she had in her shared apartment. From this point forward, Charlotte would be sleeping in his bed.

Austin wasn't surprised to find the bed empty when he

and Charlotte returned a few minutes later. Israel rarely slept with anyone—hell, he required less sleep than anyone Austin knew and rarely slept for more than a few hours, no matter how exhausted he was.

I wanted to give you time alone with your new mate, brother. I'm going to make a few calls—I had a strange dream about Catalina last night, and I can't get her out of my mind.

Israel's concern sent an arrow of alarm through Austin—he'd learned a long time ago to trust his younger brother's instincts and made a mental note to make a few calls himself. Settling his sleepy mate against his chest, Austin wrapped his arms around her and felt a wave of warm contentment crash over him. Smiling when she wiggled her ass closer, pressing against his rapidly inflating erection, Austin heard her sharp gasp of surprise.

"Don't start something you aren't going to be awake to finish, baby. You'll find shifters have incredible sexual stamina—I could fuck you all night long and still push you against the wall for a quickie first thing tomorrow morning—but you, sweet witch, need your rest because I have something special planned for you tomorrow." He felt her uncertainty for a few seconds before her breathing leveled out and knew she'd fallen asleep.

Pulling in a deep breath, Austin let his mind clear of everything but a midnight run in the woods. He'd never been able to teleport his physical being like his brother, Cleveland, but he'd always been able to send his mind to another place. Letting his senses register the memory brought the sensations back in a flood of sweet familiarity. The freedom of having the wind ruffling his fur and bringing with it all the scents of the wooded area surrounding the lake, calmed him in the way nothing else could. At this point in the mating process, sex would energize him, and his mate needed her rest. Taking a deep breath, Austin focused on running through the woods.

"I hope you burn off some of your mental energy because I need to get some sleep." Charlotte's whispered words made him smile as he tightened his arms around her, grazing his teeth along the top of her shoulder, making her shudder.

Mine!

PARIS ADLER STOOD with her hands on her hips, staring at the mountain of a man standing in front of her. Trinity Stone looked entirely different out of uniform, but the casual clothing hadn't done a thing to make him less of an ass.

"This isn't your jurisdiction, Sheriff Stone. Hell, we aren't even in the United States... what makes you think you can boss me around?" She was going to kick her sister's ass for making her travel with Mr. Bossy. Damn and double damn, there was no reason they needed to travel together. As London's maid of honor, Paris wanted to arrive ahead of everyone else to ensure everything was ready. Why anyone thought she needed the bodyguard from hell was a mystery to her.

"My concern for your safety isn't tied to my uniform. It might surprise you to learn, I'm concerned about your welfare." In her limited dealings with Trinity Stone, she'd seen him as uncompromising, but something about his rigid posture made her think there was more to his worry than he was telling her.

"Why are you really here, Sheriff Stone?" When she sensed he was about to give her a canned answer, Paris shook her head. "Let me save you the effort... as the youngest of ten, I can spot PCBS from a thousand paces. Don't give me the canned version my siblings have scripted for you. Tell me the truth." She wasn't going to tell him how easily she'd know if he was lying. As far as Paris knew, she'd only gotten two gifts from her magical parents. Paris always knew instinctively if someone was lying, and she was a magnet for children. Trinity crossed his massive arms over his chest, studying her for long seconds before sighing.

"I tried to tell Cooper you wouldn't cooperate, but he wouldn't listen."

"Cooper? Cooper Hicks? Since when does he have this kind of power in my life? Damn, like having nine siblings and three future brothers-in-law isn't enough, now I've got a former CIA agent meddling in my business?" *Isn't this just fucking dandy? Why am I always the last to know when the Everyone Who is the Boss of Paris List is being expanded?*

"Just because he's got a stiffy for my sister doesn't mean he's automatically granted power in my life." She wanted to snarl her frustration at the amusement she saw dancing in Trinity's eyes.

"A stiffy? What are you, thirteen?" Fuck a neon blue duck she wanted to slap that smirk off his face.

"Okay, I'll play." *He's evidently forgotten I have nine older brothers and sisters. I know how this works.* "Just because Cooper is fucking my sister, doesn't make him the boss of me."

Crossing her arms beneath her ample breasts, making sure they lifted toward the man fighting to keep his eyes on her face, Paris smiled to herself at the flare of his nostrils. Her brothers might not think she'd paid attention during their high school dating years, but she knew exactly what Trinity's reaction meant. He might be fighting his attraction to her, but his body was giving him away.

"Don't be crude, Sprite, it doesn't suit you."

"I'm not a sprite! They are ornery fairies, and I'm not either of those things." She liked this nickname better than *brat*, but she wasn't about to tell him so.

"You are." The damned man was over six and a half feet tall, but she'd have sworn he grew taller right before her eyes. "Sprites are fast, and you're going to lose any argument you can conceivably voice about that." The damned man knew she couldn't dispute the fact she liked to drive fast since he'd written her speeding tickets both times she'd visited the small town where he lived. He finally sighed and shook his head.

"Listen, I'm not trying to tell you how to carry out your Maid of Honor duties. I am, however, telling you there is a reason for the change in travel plans and accommodations. And… I *will* accompany you anytime you leave this suite. This is not open to negotiation, Sprite."

Staring at Trinity for long moments, Paris finally felt her body sag in surrender. "I don't know Cooper Hicks well, but living in San Diego, I've met several Navy SEALs, and I've never known them to be alarmists." Taking a deep breath, she studied the sheriff for any clue about what was going on, but his stone-faced expression wasn't giving anything away. *Fine. Whatever. I have shit to do, I don't have time to argue with a statue.*

"Okay, fine. Let's go, but I'm warning you, if you start mucking up my plans, you are history. I'll ditch you in a New York minute... and don't think I can't because I've been dealing with bossy babysitters my whole life. At this point, I have a Ph.D. in vanishing."

Stomping past him to yank open the door with as much dramatic flair as she could manage, Paris heard him mutter, "Try it, and I'll paddle your delectable ass, Sprite." Paris felt a rush of heat move through her in response to his words, but she shoved it aside. *Frick-fracking hell, I'm not attracted to him... I refuse to be attracted to a bully with a ticket book.*

"I NEED MORE coffee... and clothes... and panties. How can you possibly expect me to travel without panties? It's indecent." Charlotte stomped up the stairs, took one look at the inside of the Adler Oil jet and froze. "Wow. This is amazing. I didn't see this coming." Maybe if she'd had a second, third, or fourth cup of coffee, she might have considered the fact their jet wouldn't look anything like the few commercial flights she'd taken.

Nope, it's the panties... that's the problem. If I had on panties, my brain would work.

"Keep up the snark, and you're going to see how pleased your Master is I didn't let you hide those spankable cheeks, sweetness. We have plenty of time for a punishment session, and personally, I would enjoy working off some energy since I didn't get to run last night." Israel had been speaking over her shoulder, but when she didn't respond, he gently pushed her forward. It didn't take a rocket scientist to see Israel was deliberately baiting her.

I may not be fully functioning this morning, but I'm not entirely dim either. I'm not walking into that trap.

"Charlotte, the members of our flight crew are all part of our pack—seeing your bare ass draped over my knee will not shock them."

She spun around quickly, finger raised to make a point but snapped her mouth shut when she saw the foreboding look on Austin's face. *Damn it, when did they switch places?* Turning to a young woman dressed in a uniform, Austin nodded.

"Rebecca, my mate is in desperate need of coffee—a lot of coffee." The woman smiled at Charlotte before ducking behind a curtain.

Austin took her elbow and led her to what looked like a small seating group centered around a round table she guessed was used to conduct business meetings during flights. One wall was lined with several large computer monitors tuned to various news stations. There were several closed doors, and Charlotte wondered what laid on the other side. Austin leaned close to fasten her seat belt and licked the shell of her ear.

"One of those doors leads to our bedroom, my sweet mate. It will take us approximately eight hours to reach our destination, including a refueling stop in Miami. Since it's almost time for lunch, we'll eat, play a bit, then rest before landing in St. Barth's."

Taking a deep breath, Charlotte knew too well the details of the resort where London Adler's wedding was scheduled to take place in a few days. As Austin's Administrative Assistant, she'd helped coordinate some of the details in his absence.

"The upgrades to our reservations have been confirmed." Israel's amused tone caught her attention.

"What was wrong with what I helped arrange? Does London know you're making changes? Brides get crazy when you start mucking with stuff. This is going to be on you, I'm not going down on this one." Forgetting Austin had already fastened her safety belt, Charlotte found herself struggling against the unforgiving strap as she tried to stand.

"Stop struggling and stay where I put you, baby." Turning his attention to his grinning brother, Austin frowned. "And you," Austin thundered as he pointed his finger at the younger Adler, "stop setting her up. You don't need an excuse to spank her, you know. We'll show her how much she'll enjoy an erotic spanking after we eat lunch."

Charlotte gulped the coffee she'd been served to try to quell the surge of desire Austin's words elicited. She could feel moisture coating her sex in response to the mental picture his words painted in her mind.

Fuck me, I hope there isn't a wet spot on this seat when I stand up.

Chapter Thirteen

CHARLOTTE STOOD ON the patio of the villa, watching the waves lap the white sand beach, wishing she'd spent more time napping during the flight and less time staring at the ceiling worrying. Her dad had called twice to tell her she needed to refocus on her priorities. When she'd asked him what he thought those were, everything on his list had been about Cedar Bayou and what he wanted her to accomplish.

It was shocking how much her outlook had changed in the short time she'd been working for Austin. Keeping her secluded in the bayou meant her family's small corner of the world was all that mattered. Now, exposed to a wide variety of people with varied interests, Charlotte understood how selfish her family had been. The more she thought about it, the angrier she became. She'd been homeschooled by a variety of magicals before completing her college degrees online.

Why did you keep me locked away for so long? What's wrong with me?

Warm arms wrapped around her from behind, pulling her back against a rock-hard chest. By now, Charlotte could tell her mate from his brother by scent alone. Leaning back into his embrace, she tried to clear her mind and focus on enjoying her surroundings. She didn't want her frustration to put a damper on the Adler's family celebration.

"You've read enough about the lifestyle to understand the importance of honesty, Charlotte. I'll allow you some leeway while you are learning the rules of a D/s relationship, but that won't include withholding information—whether it relates to your safety or your happiness. I won't tolerate anything except complete transparency, mate." Austin pulled her around before tilting her chin up, forcing her to meet his gaze. Dark eyes studied her with a singular focus Charlotte knew had made him such a successful businessman. The calloused pads of his fingers tucked a stray curl behind her ear before he pressed a butterfly kiss to the center of her forehead.

"Talk to me, Charlotte. From the moment I claimed you, your physical and emotional well-being became my priority. I caught fleeting pieces of your thoughts, but I'd like for you to fill in the gaps." He'd requested rather than compelling her to explain. As the leader of his pack, Austin could have easily used his compelling voice, leaving her no choice but to answer with unvarnished honesty. But he'd asked, and that raised her respect for the man she was rapidly falling in love with.

Explaining she was beginning to question her parents' motives, particularly her dad's, wasn't easy. Austin didn't say anything as she spoke, listening without judgment made admitting how naïve she'd been seemed less painful. Charlotte wasn't sure how long they stood there, but by the time the conversation was finished, she felt as if a weight had been lifted from her shoulders.

"Thank you for being so candid, Little Star, I'm sure that wasn't easy." The breeze moving silently down the water's edge lifted her curls, making them dance around her face. Austin smoothed the wayward strands back, trapping them at her nape. "I met your father once a long time ago, but since I don't know him well, I can't comment on his motives, but I do want to say this—and Charlotte, I want you to listen closely. Nobody is going to use you or take advantage of your magical skills while I'm alive. I know I've explained your happiness and safety are my priority, and I'm going to keep telling you until I'm convinced you believe it to the bottom of your soul."

IT WAS TAKING every ounce of energy Austin could spare to block his anger. He didn't want Charlotte to misunderstand and blame herself for the tidal wave of frustration building inside him. Sharing his questions with Israel had been easy and knowing his brother would ask all the right questions reassured Austin he'd have the answers soon.

Eamon Sumner may carry a name meaning *summoner and protector*, but Austin suspected Charlotte's father was more interested in protecting his community than his own flesh and blood. He hoped like hell the man, who would someday be his father-in-law, was simply unaware of how hurt his daughter felt by his actions—time would tell.

Austin needed a few minutes alone to calm down and walking barefoot down the beach would give him a chance to absorb some of the calming energy of the sea. Shifters and other magicals are earthbound, deriving strength from the connection. Every magical text he'd ever read included reminders about the importance of sinking your hands or feet into the earth.

"Charlotte, Paris is on her way over. She'd like to go over some of the wedding details with you—well, I think her exact words were closer to wanting to talk to someone with an appreciation for romantic details, but I didn't take the bait." Austin appreciated his brother's impeccable timing—Israel's humor was the perfect segue, and he suspected his youngest sister had been more than happy to help.

"Go ahead, baby. I'm happy you'll have the opportunity to spend some time with Paris. It will be good for her to have the inside scoop, for a change. As the youngest, she often feels left out of the loop." It was true, Paris felt forgotten most of the time—hell, he had only recently begun making a concerted effort to include her. He was still scratching his head and wondering when had his youngest sibling turned into such a beautiful young woman.

Walking the few steps to the beach after Israel led Charlotte inside, Austin let his bare feet sink into the soft sand, standing perfectly still for several minutes, allowing Mother Nature's power seep into his system. He didn't plan to walk far from their villa—this soon after mating, any significant distance between mates was difficult to endure. He may have needed time to rein in his irritation, but he wouldn't stray far. Austin's wolf felt the vibration of another magical, making all his senses more acute.

"It's always impossible to sneak up on a shifter, their animal instincts are far too keen." Glancing to his side,

Austin knew immediately who stood at his side, even if the elderly man was hiding behind a much younger façade. Whether Audric Stafford was the most skilled wizard in the world was open to debate, but he was without question the most politically powerful. "You don't look surprised to see me, Austin. Let me guess, my lovely Brigitte has already dropped in on her beloved niece."

"Yes, she dropped by very quickly after Charlotte and I were mated." If his mate's grandfather thought he'd be easily intimidated, he hadn't done his homework.

"I'm not here to comment on the circumstances of your mating with Charlotte. In fact, I believe the two of you will be a powerful force in the future. I wanted to fill in a few blanks for you and congratulate my granddaughter." Without giving Austin an opportunity to respond, the other man continued speaking without looking away from the water.

"My son-in-law loves his daughter. He doesn't always show it in ways I find acceptable, but I've never had any reason to question his devotion to her."

Austin turned to the other man, hoping his doubt was clearly reflected in his expression so he wouldn't have to put it into words. He was still struggling to bring his frustration back to a manageable level and arguing with the Minister of Magic wasn't in anyone's best interest.

"Amaya was always a sucker for handsome, charismatic men. I'm shocked she hasn't already stopped by to meet you." When Austin frowned, the other man chuckled. "I have no illusions when it comes to my daughters, Austin. They both love men—even though they see their partners in different roles."

Austin couldn't hold back his laughter. He'd only seen

Amaya Sumner once, several years earlier at a meeting, but he hadn't gotten the impression she was a Domme. For the first time since Charlotte's grandfather showed up, Austin relaxed.

"Charlotte's magic will fully manifest now that she's mated."

"Does she know?" It wasn't unusual for certain magicals to come more fully into their magic after mating, but since Charlotte already had numerous impressive magical abilities, he doubted she would be expecting a significant change.

"No. None of us know exactly what's going to happen, and that includes the other members of the Council. What I do know is the agents from your government are watching her closely. Now that you've claimed her, she is much more vulnerable."

"Explain."

Goddess, Austin was never going to get himself under control at this rate. Hell, he was going to end up with high blood pressure by the end of the damned week. Surprisingly, Audric's explanation made perfect sense. Anyone planning to tap into her magical skills would want them as fully developed as possible, and it wouldn't take much research of the ancient writings to learn a mated magical would acquire additional skills, or any skills they possessed would be enhanced.

"Are you telling me Charlotte is in danger of being kidnapped by the United States government?" Austin didn't consider himself naïve, but it was difficult to believe their own leaders would kidnap American citizens. The look the elderly man gave him made it clear the Council Chief did indeed think Austin was dangerously naïve.

"You have well-placed friends. Don't hesitate to call on them, let them help you protect our sweet Charlotte. The Universe has amazing things planned for her. Your job will be to help keep her safe from the people who would use her powers for nefarious purposes."

Goddess, I didn't know anyone used that word anymore. Israel's sarcasm whispered through Austin's mind, forcing him to bite the insides of his mouth to keep from laughing.

"My friends are already aware there is an issue. They'll rally around Charlotte because she is now one of their own. I'll do everything I can to keep her safe, but I want you to know I'll never turn down help." Austin wanted the Audric to know Charlotte's safety was more important than his pride.

When the other man turned to face him, Austin got a glimpse of the man Charlotte knew as her grandfather as opposed to the Council of Magic Chairman. Despite his magical disguise, the eyes of an old soul softened with affection.

"I'll pop back over after your sister's wedding. It will give me an opportunity to congratulate the happy trio and give my granddaughter a quick blessing as well." Grinning, he answered Austin's unasked question.

"I've been vacationing at a St. Maarten resort for the past several weeks… there are a lot of single ladies my age, well, this age." He waved at his new look and winked. Austin leaned his head back, laughing. When he straightened, the man was gone. *Damn wizards.*

PARIS BREEZED INTO her brothers' villa and ran straight into Israel's waiting arms. "Hello, brother mine. I have missed you so much." She made no attempt to hold back her giggle when he twirled her around, just as all her brothers had for as long as she could remember. In her peripheral vision, Paris saw Trinity Stone greeting Austin's assistant, Charlotte Hays.

"I missed you too, Imp. Austin will be back in a couple of minutes." Paris was dying to ask him what was up, but his quick glance to where Charlotte stood, told her he wasn't going to answer her questions in front of Ms. Hays. "You've met, Charlotte?" When she nodded, Israel turned his attention to Sheriff Stone, making quick work of the introductions, giving the other woman a brief overview of Cooper's request for Trinity to become her damned shadow. Moving forward to greet Charlotte, Paris grinned.

"Cooper better have a damned good reason for torturing me." Charlotte's brows peaked before she turned to Trinity.

"Are you torturing Ms. Adler, Sheriff? I can't imagine her brothers being happy knowing their precious baby sister is being tormented and think of the political ramifications. I can see the headline in your hometown newspaper now... Beautiful Young Woman Verbally Brutalized by Local Sheriff." There was no mistaking Charlotte's mocking tone and the upward quirk of her lips. Paris couldn't hold back her laughter.

"Damn, I like you already. We're going to be great friends. I think we should make you an honorary Adler." If Charlotte's blush hadn't let Paris know there was a story to sniff out, Israel's bark of laughter certainly would have.

"This time, you are going to be the first—well, second if you count Israel, to know some very juicy family gossip, Sweet Pea." Austin made a mental note to remind Asia to pretend this was news. Austin was the only one of Paris' brothers who called her by the same endearment her dad had always used, and it never failed to make her heart smile despite the loss.

"Charlotte and I are already mated, Paris."

Speechless, Paris stared, unblinking, at her eldest brother for several silent seconds. Holy freaking cats, she was *SPEECHLESS*… and everybody knew how unusual that was. Paris knew her mouth was hanging open, her eyes wide as saucers when she was finally able to move her gaze from Austin to Charlotte before her gaze returned to her brother.

"I don't want this shared with the rest of the family until after the newlyweds leave for their honeymoon. The next couple of days are London's, I don't want to steal any of her thunder."

Paris launched herself into her brother's arms, hugging him so tight, her arms ached from the effort. "You are the *bestest*. I hope someday I find someone as sweet as Charlotte." Austin tightened his arms around her and pressed a kiss against her temple before speaking softly against her ear.

"Sweet Pea, I'm looking forward to telling the man who captures your heart that he is the luckiest bastard in the world."

Chapter Fourteen

CHARLOTTE GROANED AS Austin pushed his cock balls deep in her slick heat. She'd enjoyed getting to know Paris and Trinity—in her opinion, the two of them were fighting a losing battle resisting their obvious attraction. Watching them snipe at each other, she'd realized the verbal sparring was nothing more than foreplay.

The bride and grooms were on their way but wouldn't arrive at the resort until late tonight, so everyone was enjoying a bit of downtime before the festivities began in earnest. The growing group planned to have breakfast together, then split up until dinner. Charlotte yelped when a sharp slap landed on her right ass cheek.

"A new rule for you, sweet mate. If we are in a scene or I have my cock in you, I expect to have your undivided attention."

Shit! I have to remember he can listen in on my thoughts or learn to block him… I wonder if I could do that?

"You could, but I would know, and if you start using magic between us, I can do the same."

The tip of his cock nudged her womb, and despite the obvious distraction, she understood what he was telling her. Charlotte suspected Austin hadn't used his compelling voice on her out of respect and because he truly believed in safe, sane, and consensual. But if she started blocking him, all bets would be off.

Grazing his teeth along the top of her shoulder, Austin paused for several seconds before thrusting so hard, she nearly fell forward. She loved how the ridges of his cock rubbed the walls of her vagina, his tip pushing against her cervix. And when she was on all fours, she always felt the warm splash of his cum against her womb. Someday soon, they would talk about starting a family, but she needed to finish school first and find a job that allowed her to use the education she'd worked so hard to finish.

AUSTIN HAD WARNED Charlotte about her focus, but her quick mind was still spinning out of control. He wasn't surprised—so much had changed in her life in a remarkably short period of time, he was damned impressed she was handling things as well as she was. But he had news for her—she would be finishing her education sooner rather than later.

Austin knew he had to replace her as his assistant, not because of any company rule against nepotism, but because he wouldn't get a damned thing done if she was readily available. Hell, there wasn't a drilling or shipping problem in the world that would hold his attention if he caught a whiff of her pussy's tempting honey.

Biting down hard enough to make her gasp, but without breaking the skin, Austin growled against her ear, "Hang on, Little Star, I'm going to fuck you hard and fast.

You have permission to come." Without waiting for her response, Austin canted his hips, pulling his cock halfway out of her hot channel, then shoving himself back in so deep, he felt her heartbeat.

"You are mine, Charlotte. Mine to love. Mine to protect. Mine to fuck."

He emphasized each point with increasingly sharp pinches to her exposed clit and groaned when she shouted his name. The walls of her vagina squeezed him so tightly, Austin was unable to hold back his own release. Feeling his seed splash back against the sensitive head of his cock ramped up the intensity of his orgasm to the point Austin saw stars dancing behind his eyelids.

The taut muscles in his arms started to quiver from the isometric strain, making him worry they might not hold his considerable weight—the last thing he wanted to do was fall on her. With an agonized groan, Austin made a concerted effort to remember his mate was petite by any standard and rolled to the side—it was easy to forget how small Charlotte was because her personality was so large.

"You turned my brain to mush. I wanted to go to the beach and swim this afternoon, but I'm not sure I can get my arms and legs to move, let alone work together. Hell, I'd probably drown in the bathtub at this point." Austin would have laughed at her sass if he'd had any oxygen to spare.

"I'll go with you to the beach as soon as I can move. I've been looking forward to swimming in the ocean again." Austin loved the beach. As the oldest, he'd gotten to enjoy more of his parents' travels than his siblings. They'd roamed the world, but it wasn't the amazing tourist destinations that stood out in his memory, it was the time they'd spent walking along sandy shores. It hadn't mattered to Austin if it was hotter than Hades or if their walk was under a moonlit sky, he'd loved the energy he felt vibrating from each frothy wave as it kissed the coast.

"Let's eat a snack before we go. That will give Israel time to finish his errands." Letting his lips linger along her jawline, pressing butterfly kisses in a line to her ear, he continued, "We have plans for you, Little Star." He and Israel had already planned to play with her under the new moon. "The Caribbean sky is known for its brilliant array of stars, and the lack of moonlight will make them look like brilliant diamonds on black velvet, but you, Little Star, will outshine them all."

CATALINA LEANED BACK against the lounger, letting the Caribbean sunshine warm her tired muscles. She hadn't been surprised to learn Cooper had arranged for the two of them to share a villa at the end of a row occupied by the Adler clan. She'd planned to share a villa with Asia and Paris, but Cooper had changed all the arrangements, ensuring each of them had a bodyguard. Knowing he was worried about her sisters becoming collateral damage due to the threats to her safety was humbling, but she was grateful he was working to protect her family.

The tinkling of an iced drink caused her to open her eyes to thank the wide-eyed concierge who stood at the end of her lounger as a waiter gave her a quick bow without making eye contact. Returning her gaze to the man studying her, she could sense his hesitance. She finally gave him a tired smile which he evidently took as permission to engage her in conversation.

"Ms. Adler, I hope I'm not overstepping any boundaries, but I want you to know we have medical staff on site should you need them."

She knew he had her best interests at heart and appreciated his concern, but she'd had all the damned medical attention she wanted to endure for a very long time. Cat knew what he was seeing... the deep purple bruises along her ribs on both sides of a battered torso and over a hundred stitches, closing cuts on her upper arms and thighs. Her bikini didn't cover much, but thank the great Goddess, it covered the bite and pinch marks on her breasts.

"Thanks so much, but I was just released from a hospital in California." She didn't like lying when it wasn't strictly necessary, but if he decided to do a bit of research, he might inadvertently give away her location to the men who'd ordered her kidnapping. Searching stateside should keep him from getting any hits since she'd been using an alias during her mission in Indonesia, and she'd been registered in the Frankfurt hospital as Mrs. Catherine Hicks.

"Understood. Should you change your mind, I'm here to help, and I can assure you, your privacy is always a priority."

Nodding, Cat fought back the wave of emotion his compassion brought to the surface. Her doctors had warned her she might experience mood swings as a part of her recovery, but she'd been unprepared for how wide her emotional pendulum would swing.

"No need to respond, Miss. You aren't the first guest we've had who has experienced violence. It's a point of pride for us to play a small role in our guest's recovery. Don't underestimate the potential and symptoms of Post-Traumatic Stress Disorder. It can sneak up on you."

Catalina had the feeling he was speaking more from experience than observation, but she kept it to herself. Fucking hell, the more compassion he showed, the harder it was to hold back her tears. Feeling Cooper's hand on her shoulder, Cat let out the breath she hadn't realized she was holding.

"Thanks, Evander. I haven't had a chance to brief Ms. Adler about your background yet. I'd be willing to bet she thinks you are our villa's concierge."

Cat would have turned to glare at Cooper if she'd been able to twist her torso. Damned man knew she couldn't turn around.

The man in front of her smiled, the change taking years off his appearance. "Cooper and I worked together a few times, but I was lucky enough to leave Spies R Us behind—family obligations and all that. As for your concierge, I'll be dropping by occasionally, but at Cooper's request, you won't have anyone else in your villa full-time."

The pain medication she'd taken a few minutes ago finally kicking in, Catalina pulled her sunglasses down her nose and blinked furiously, trying to bring the well-dressed man back into focus.

"I'm confused. I thought Captain America back here was all about securing sh… I mean, he was working with my brothers to make certain nobody had enough space to breathe. If you aren't part of the bodyguard squad, why are you here?" For the first time, she saw the light of amusement in his eyes a split second before he leaned his head back and laughed.

"Brother, you have met your match—and it's about damned time." Moving to her side, the man Cooper called Evander knelt next to her, taking her hand in his. "I own the resort, Catalina. I returned to take over when my dad died suddenly. What I discovered was a property run down to the point it was barely salvageable, teetering on the brink of bankruptcy."

"Princess, Evander rebuilt this place in under a year. The resort's reputation as a safe haven for those needing privacy—either for their event or because they need a place to heal—is second to none. Your sister and her fiancés could not have chosen a better place for their wedding. Not only is Evander well-trained, his security would make Cam Barnes and Ian McGregor green with envy."

"I've been fortunate to be able to call in some favors." Evander chuckled and shrugged his shoulders, giving her hand a soft squeeze before setting it gently back on the edge of the lounger. "We've added a few extra gadgets to all the villas your family is using this week, but this one is wired for movement around the perimeter of the unit itself as an added precaution. We want you to feel safe here, Catalina."

Cat's eyes burned with unshed tears, making it difficult to squeeze words of thanks past the knot in her throat. She was grateful for everything Cooper had done—he'd saved her life, gotten her onto a plane without any documentation, and into an American military hospital without anyone asking questions.

Catalina knew how lucky she was to be alive, and once she recovered, she planned to find whoever had sold her out. She wouldn't be truly safe until she knew who was behind her kidnapping. Even though the men who'd held her hadn't appeared to know she was anything more than an American jewelry designer, Cat was convinced whoever had given the order knew exactly who he was dealing with.

Until she found out who was after her, Cat wouldn't be safe… and neither would anyone she cared about. Knowing she was endangering her family by attending London's wedding made her heart skip a beat. Damn, she really needed to get out of here. There had to be another resort nearby, perhaps on a nearby island. She could rent a boat and return just long enough to attend the ceremony, then leave again right away. No doubt Evan and Eli Monroe selected this resort because it was not only stunning but safe.

Shaking her head, Cat still couldn't believe her sister was marrying not one but two shifters. Catalina had been a part of the lifestyle long enough to know ménage marriages were more common than most people were aware, but her younger sister was still going to face a lot of questioning looks. Smiling to herself, Cat had to admit London was the last one of the Adler sisters she'd expected to go such an unconventional route.

"Cat? Catalina? Princess, you need to come back to me."

The gentle stroking of Cooper's fingers up and down the sensitive skin along the inside of her bare arm finally cut through the worried static of her thoughts. Blinking several times, she brought herself back to the moment. Giving Cooper a wane smile, Catalina knew she was fighting a losing battle against a tidal wave of fatigue.

"Come on, Princess, you need to rest. I don't want you falling asleep out here and getting a sunburn. It's going to be hard enough to find a dress to hide the bruises without adding a painful sunburn to the equation."

As Cooper carried her into the villa, she heard the other man promise to find her some long-sleeved shirts and long skirts. Cat barely registered the cool caress of high-end sheets against her back as he settled her on the bed. Slipping into the blissful darkness, Cat let go, knowing Cooper would keep her safe.

Chapter Fifteen

CHARLOTTE WAS GRATEFUL she'd met most of the men and women on the veranda because it would have been difficult to keep the various members of the boisterous crew straight otherwise. Despite the chaos, she noticed Kensington and Cleveland hadn't arrived yet. Wondering what their plans were, she pulled her phone from the pocket of her dress and began checking messages. She'd just opened a text from one of the assistants in the office when a large hand wrapped around her phone, pulling it from her hands.

"If my brother sees you working, he'll paddle your sweet ass... then I'll pull you over my knee and add a few swats of my own." Israel powered off her phone before pushing it into his pocket. Nodding his head toward the side, he grinned. "Bronx is worse than you are, but it will be Asia who busts him, watch and see." Before his prediction could be fulfilled, Charlotte watched a beautiful woman enter on the arm of a man she hadn't met.

Recognizing the woman as Austin's younger sister, Catalina, Charlotte made her way to where the two newcomers stood. Austin wrapped his arm around Charlotte's shoulders as she stepped forward to welcome them to the party. Catalina stepped into her brother's arms, and Austin's gentle hug seemed at odds with the way he'd greeted his other sisters. Charlotte wondered why he was treating Catalina as if she were made of spun glass until he turned the other woman to her and grinned. After a quick greeting, Catalina introduced Cooper Hicks, then reached out to gently wrap her arms around Charlotte.

The pain slammed into Charlotte's chest like a sledge-hammer, stealing her breath and making her eyes water. Catalina started to step away, but Charlotte didn't let her go. Holding her close, Charlotte focused her magic on the battered woman, taking the pain as her own and healing the cuts and contusions she knew were hidden by her clothing. Catalina sighed as she sagged against Charlotte. Taking a deep breath, Charlotte turned into Austin's waiting arms when she felt him pull her out of his sister's embrace.

"What the fuck was that?" Cooper held Catalina in his arms, staring at Charlotte with something between wonder and horror. "You've got the same injuries Catalina suffered in... holy shit, they're disappearing."

Charlotte looked down to see the cuts healing quickly as she'd known they would. She knew from experience the internal injuries would take longer to heal, but by morning, all traces of Catalina's physical injuries would be gone... but it was the emotional toll she knew would be harder to erase. Charlotte sagged against Austin for several minutes before she realized Israel was pressed against her other side. Catalina stood nearby, her eyes shining with unshed tears.

"Come on, Little Star, they're ready to serve dinner."

"I've alerted Evander, he's bringing Charlotte a change of clothes from our villa."

Luckily, the events of the last several minutes had gone largely unnoticed by the other guests. Fifteen minutes later, Charlotte had added a light sweater, hiding the fading bruises. She sat silently between Austin and Israel while London and her men thanked everyone for joining them for the coming festivities. Cooper and Catalina sat across from them, watching her closely, questions dancing in their eyes.

"I want everyone to remember, the next few days are about London, Evan, and Eli. I don't want anything to spoil their celebration." When Catalina started to speak, Austin shook his head. "After dinner, we'll go back to our villa and talk—until then, let's enjoy the party."

TWO HOURS LATER, Catalina stepped into the villa her brothers and Charlotte occupied, kicked off her shoes, and headed to the bar where Evander stood waiting. She had never worked with the former agent, but that didn't mean she didn't know his story. Like every other *company* employee who *retired*, he hadn't been able to completely cut his ties with the agency. With Eli and Evan Monroe's connections, she wasn't surprised they'd chosen Evander's resort as the venue for their wedding. From what she'd learned from Cooper during dinner, the exclusive resort was known among operatives as a safe haven.

"You look much better, Catalina. Your family appears to have been very good for you." He set a crystal tumbler on the bar in front of her and smiled. "Sparkling water before anything stronger since you didn't drink enough with your dinner." She could only shake her head and laugh, not surprised he'd noticed she'd been too distracted to eat or drink much during their meal.

"Thanks, I was too stunned to focus on the amazing dinner your staff prepared." She let her eyes roam around the large common area before focusing on the wall of glass facing the ocean. She watched a member of Evander's staff slide the floor to ceiling glass panels back until the two areas melded together creating a huge indoor/outdoor living space. She wasn't surprised her brothers had chosen a villa at the end, affording them the privacy she knew both Austin and Israel craved. Its proximity to the lapping waves would infuse the eldest Adler with the energy he always sought at the beach.

Austin had always jumped at any opportunity to visit an ocean beach. Smiling to herself, she wondered how long it would be before he bought his own Caribbean beach home. Cooper stepped up to the bar, silently motioning Evander to the side. After a short discussion, the two men moved back to where she waited.

Charlotte walked gingerly into the room at the same time Cat opened her mouth to ask what the two of them had been gossiping about. Getting to her feet, Cat moved out to the deck where Austin was settling his assistant on a well-padded, wicker sofa. Catalina had been watching the intimacy of Austin and Charlotte's body language all evening—it was easy to see they were more than co-workers.

"Start talking big brother... and I want to know everything... from the beginning." Catalina had always been direct, but tonight the stakes were even higher. Fuck polite, she wanted the story... and she wanted it now.

"Anybody who thinks the oldest child is the most annoying and pushy has never met my sisters." Austin's grumbling was negated by the chaste kiss he pressed to the top of Catalina's head. "What we're going to tell you does not leave this villa until after the newlyweds are off the island." Cat recognized that tone. Her brother was determined to keep everyone's focus on London during the next few days.

"Good Goddess, if this keeps up, it's going to be the worst kept secret in history." Israel rolled his eyes as he settled on Charlotte's free side before handing her what looked like a frozen margarita.

"Hey, Evander, why does Charlotte get a real drink and got water?" She glared at the man leaning against the base of a swaying palm tree, wondering when he'd moved outside.

"Don't blame, Evander. Look at your glass, Princess. It still has water in it. You aren't getting anything stronger until you're hydrated."

Before dinner, she wouldn't have had the strength to argue with Cooper, but now... oh yeah, bring it, Ace. She was all ready to remind Cooper he wasn't the boss of her when she met Charlotte's gaze and realized the other woman was minutes from imploding.

"Shit, I'm sorry, Charlotte, my whining is keeping you from getting the rest you obviously need. My brothers can fill in the back story later. Please tell me what the hell happened during that hug because I've never experienced anything like it." Catalina listened as Charlotte recounted she'd learned at an early age how to heal others by taking their injuries as her own. The longer Charlotte talked, but more obvious it became Austin's unassuming assistant hadn't fully recovered from the internal injuries.

"How long does it usually take you to recover?" Catalina was humbled to know the other woman had willingly taken on her pain. The pink stain on Charlotte's cheeks made Cat sit up a little straighter as she waited for the answer.

"It's never taken this long, I usually recover very quickly, but your injuries..." Charlotte looked from Cat to the men surrounding them before giving Catalina a sad smile. "I'll be okay by morning, but I'm worried about you."

The backs of Cat's eyes burned as she realized the woman sitting in front of her knew what she'd been through. Charlotte had not only taken Cat's physical injuries as her own, she'd seen into Catalina's soul, seeing the pain and fear she hadn't shared with anyone else. For the first time since Cooper carried her out of that dark hellhole, Catalina let herself cry.

AUSTIN STOOD ON the stone patio, watching the waves crash against the sandy shore. He'd let Israel carry Charlotte to bed, knowing if he carried her anywhere near a bed, he'd never have enough self-control to walk away. Sensing his sister approaching, Austin lifted his arm, letting her step close enough, he could feel the heat of her body. Wrapping his arm around her, Austin pulled Catalina against his side.

"Cooper called me minutes before he stormed that damned compound and promised he was going to bring you home to us, Cat. I don't think I've ever been more scared in my entire life. Knowing you'd been kidnapped was bad enough, but hearing the experts tell me how often victims are killed before the cavalry can get to them was terrifying." It had nearly killed him to keep the secret from their siblings, but Austin had given Cooper his word. Taking a steadying breath, Austin looked down into her eyes.

"Stay home for a while, Cat. Hell, I don't think my heart can take you going out on another mission soon. My mate just put her own health on the line to help you, little sister. I'd hate to think it was wasted effort."

"Mate?"

Austin should have known to cover his damned ears, hell, he'd grown up with five sisters, for Goddess' sake. As a shifter, his enhanced hearing was particularly sensitive to shrill sounds, and Catalina's shriek made his ears hurt so bad, he worried they might bleed. *Damn, I should have seen that coming.*

"Does anyone besides Israel know? Paris knows, doesn't she? There is no way she could be around the two of you and not ask questions, and Goddess knows, you wouldn't lie to her. Fucking hell, there will be no living with her now. She will lord this over the rest of us forever." Catalina grinned up at him before wrapping her arms around him, hugging him tightly.

"I'm really happy for you, big brother. You have worked so damned hard for so long, ensuring Adler Oil was a success, you deserve every ounce of happiness you can get. I'm thrilled for you, and my new sister is a total badass. Those are some mad skills she's got." Stepping back, Cat looped her arm through his, tugging him toward the villa's interior. "Come on, we need to celebrate." When he rolled his eyes, she laughed. "We'll celebrate London's upcoming nuptials. Perhaps, if I've come up with a plausible excuse, the liquor police will give me something stronger than sparkling water."

Catalina laughed as they approached the bar where Evander stood, pouring wine. Austin saw Cooper visibly relax when he saw Cat was no longer limping, her body moving with its usual fluid grace. Austin had been briefed on his sister's injuries and understood the other man's relief. Knowing the effort it had taken for Catalina to attend London's wedding week festivities was proof their parents had stressed the importance of family at every opportunity.

Austin enjoyed his guests' company but couldn't stop thinking about his mate. He looked forward to making their union legal in the eyes of the state. Their mating was sealed as far as his pack and the magic community were concerned, but he wanted to make sure they covered the legal bases as well.

"Go. You'll feel better when you can check on her yourself, and I'll rest easier knowing she has you close. I know you don't believe you have any magic other than the ability to shapeshift, but you're wrong. You took a company teetering on the edge of insolvency and turned it around under the worst possible circumstances." Cat gave him a quick hug before trailing her cool fingers down the side of his face.

Austin smiled down at the beautiful woman he called sister, awed by her courage, and sent up a silent prayer she would be a little less fearless in the future.

"I love you, big brother, and I hope like hell you to know how special you are. Who is the first person we all call when we need help? You've been our leader since it wasn't always a compliment."

Austin wasn't usually one to openly show affection, but Catalina's sincerity had him pulling her into his embrace for a tight hug before he finally let her go. Her eyes were shiny with unshed tears, making his heart clench.

"Mom always told us our magic would grow when we found our *One*. Your real magic isn't shifting, Austin. The Universe's gift to you is your ability to love and comfort. You've had a lot of practice with nine siblings... go and show Charlotte how lucky she is to belong to you.

I love you, Cat, but this time you are wrong. I'm the lucky one... hell, I'm the luckiest man on the planet.

Chapter Sixteen

C HARLOTTE LEANED BACK against the lounger, letting the warm rays of the sun penetrate her tired muscles and tried to forget she was naked. Damn, her ass cheeks were still burning from the spanking she'd gotten for what Austin and Israel called her bratty behavior. She'd defiantly explained she wasn't arguing... rather, she was simply explaining why they were wrong. Austin had promptly upended her over his knees, and the second paddling had been even more painful than the first. *Bossy bastards.*

"I assure you my mother would have resented that assessment, Little Star." Austin's voice sounded from beside her, causing her to gasp in surprise.

"It's not nice to sneak up on people nor is it nice to listen in on their thoughts. Dancing door knockers, that's a whole new level of privacy invasion. Are you sure you don't work for the CIA? You probably have one of those frequent shopper's cards for Spies-R-Us. Can you hear other people, too? Well, other than Israel? How about your other brothers and sisters? Holy hell, I'll bet you were the biggest tattle-tale in the world if you knew what they were thinking." *Makes me glad I was an only child.* "I always thought my parents cheated me out of siblings, but now

I'm starting to see what a huge blessing it was."

Closing her eyes, Charlotte fought her body's reaction to Austin's proximity. Why did the man have to be sex on a fucking stick? He'd just fucked her until she'd sworn her bones melted, and her damned greedy pussy was already pulsing with need. The grin he gave her let Charlotte know he'd heard her description of him and her frustration with the growing need she felt for him.

"Your reaction is perfectly normal, Little Star. If it makes you feel any better, I'm suffering from a continual ache for you as well. I can barely think of anything except how good it feels to slide my bare cock through the heated silk of your pussy. There are moments when I don't care about anything else—fucking you is my only priority." Sighing, he took a deep breath.

"This is why newly mated couples are typically sheltered by the rest of the pack for several weeks. They are so distracted, they are vulnerable to attack. I'm sure I don't have to explain why it's a huge problem, particularly for pack leaders."

Pushing her sunglasses down her nose, Charlotte raised her brows in question. Surely, he wasn't serious.

"Dangerous because they lose all sense of decorum or because they do all their thinking with the little head? I don't have any personal experience, but I suspect the little head doesn't make the best business decisions." Damn it, why was she pushing him? Her ass was still sore, for heaven's sake. When he folded his arms over his broad chest, his body language spoke volumes. He wasn't happy with her attitude. Charlotte shrugged off her growing frustration.

"Are you going to fire me?" Fuck a fat fairy. What was wrong with her? She knew better than to blurt out questions without mulling them over. *I hate it when my mouth forgets to engage my brain before acting.* Austin dropped his arms, his pose going from rigid to understanding between one heartbeat and the next.

"Is this why you've been so difficult today? You're worried about your job?"

"Yes. No. I don't know." The tears she'd been trying to hold back for the past few days spilled down her sun-kissed cheeks. "It was an easy job... and I got to work with you." Her excuse sounded lame even to her own ears. She hadn't been his assistant long enough to do much more than making travel plans for the boss who'd been out of the office almost the entire time she'd been in the position. The truth was, she'd spoken with London more than she had Austin, and the lovely bride didn't even work for Adler Oil.

"I'm not going to fire you, but I *am* going to reassign you." Charlotte felt her eyes widen in disbelief. "Don't look so surprised, Little Star. You and I both know you are working too far below your abilities. You're already enrolled to complete your doctorate at the University of Texas Austin." Giving her a cheeky grin, he added, "I have to admit, knowing my first and last names will be on your diploma feeds my ego."

Charlotte wasn't sure what surprised her more—that he'd already taken the initiative to help her finish her Ph.D. or he'd just told her she would have his last name by the time she graduated. *If that was a proposal, it had to be the worst one in history.* Maybe shifters don't think their mates

165

need romantic proposals since from everything she'd ever heard, they considered mating the ultimate commitment.

AUSTIN LISTENED TO his sweet mate's mind spin, fighting his smile. If it was a romantic proposal she wanted, that was exactly what the future Mrs. Austin Adler would get. And she would be an Adler before she stepped through the doors of UTA's business school. Hell, he'd bet his last acquisition Israel had already enrolled her as Charlotte Adler.

"If you attend classes full-time, you'll be finished in less than a year, or you can choose a slower track and work part-time at Adler Oil. I have a special project in mind for you—whether you start on it before or after graduation is up to you."

"A special… special project? What kind of project?" He could hear the excitement building in her voice, interest practically vibrating around her.

"Seems I'm the proud owner of a magical bayou. I need to know how to develop the area, so it's both environmentally friendly and economically responsible for many years. I've heard there are some very special people who call the area home." He wasn't sure how she'd done it, but one moment she'd been sitting up on the wicker lounger, and the next, her naked body was plastered against his chest. The distinctly tropical scent of coconut oil filled his senses, and he chuckled out loud.

"Why do I have the feeling I'm going to need to send these clothes out to the cleaners?" His only consolation was the obnoxious floral shirt Evander insisted he'd needed to blend in while he looked around the small village was now thoroughly soaked with suntan oil. There's a pity. Maybe now I can change into something that doesn't scream, 'Mug me, I'm a tourist.'

"If you were naked, it wouldn't be an issue."

Austin chuckled at Charlotte's comment. His mate was getting bolder, and there was a part of him that was amused, but the sexually dominant side of his personality bristled at her blatant attempt to top from the bottom. Austin hadn't planned to push her training as his submissive until after London's wedding, but she'd just upped the stakes. Without setting her down, Austin strode confidently into the villa. Picking up the velvet box he'd left on the end of the bar, he returned outside, setting her on her feet.

"Spread your feet shoulder-width apart, bend over, and grasp your ankles." When she opened her mouth to speak, Austin frowned. "Here's a piece of advice, sub. When you find yourself in a hole—stop digging." This time she nodded slowly before following his instructions.

Using his fingers, Austin played with the slick folds, circling her clit without giving the sensitive bundle of nerves the attention her body was begging for. When Charlotte shifted position in a useless attempt to direct his touch, he gave her pussy a sharp slap. Damn, her ass was still scarlet from the spankings she'd gotten earlier. Smiling to himself, he realized she was going to have to stand up during the wedding—served her right for the sass she'd given him.

Her scent was torturing him, the sweet smell of temptation already embedded in his psyche. Austin knew he'd be able to track her with his eyes closed—his wolf would be able to find her, no matter how far she was from him. Her soft mewing sounds were growing louder, fueling his desire, sending more blood rushing to his already rigid length. When she began pushing back into his touch, Austin pulled his hand back to give her tender ass a sharp slap.

"Don't be greedy. You'll accept what you are given with gratitude." When he moved his fingers back between her legs, he pushed two small balls so deep, he knew she felt them press against her womb. He'd kept the balls in a bowl of ice until a few minutes ago; his hand had warmed the smooth surface, but it wouldn't take long before the cold liquid sloshing inside the spheres produced a unique sensation.

Charlotte's body wouldn't know which sensation to respond to—the rhythmic pressure against her vaginal walls or the cold he was sure was already sneaking up on her. He planned to leave the balls in until his sassy sub understood there were many ways to punish bad behavior. Austin looked forward to tugging on the string connecting the balls—it wouldn't take much to restart the fluid's back-and-forth motion.

"Fuck me, what did you push inside me? It's moving and freezing... and it's making me so hot."

"Do not come. Do you understand, Charlotte? You do not have permission to come."

She bit her lower lip to keep from expressing her frustration with his command. Charlotte held her tongue, but her mind was racing at warp speed. Giving her clit a quick pinch, Austin felt her body shudder under his touch. *Did she just growl at me?* Given her magical background, he'd wondered if she would someday be able to shift even though he hadn't seen any evidence of the change.

"Hold it, breathe through it. Do it for me, Little Star—because it pleases me for you to follow my commands." She sucked in several steadying breaths before he sensed she'd finally pulled herself back under control. "Good girl. Now, it's time for you get dressed. I've set out something for you to wear." Helping her stand, Austin smiled at the glassy look in her eyes.

The smallest shift in position was enough to set the balls in motion, and he heard her sharp intake of breath. Hell, she'd be lucky if she remembered attending the wedding. His brother, Kensington, had finally rolled in a few minutes ago and had already called, asking to meet Charlotte. Austin knew Israel and Kenz were close, so it was a no brainer how the most famous among the Adler siblings had heard the eldest had found his mate.

"How am I ever going to... oh, shit." Austin was shocked when her knees folded. Without his lightning-fast reflexes, she'd have crashed all the way to the concrete. Her body was trembling so hard, she was damned difficult to hold. It had been a long time since he'd completely misjudged what a submissive could tolerate. He felt like a fucking novice, and it was humbling—too fucking humbling for words.

"Come for me, mate." Charlotte's keening wail filled the air around him as her body convulsed. He knew without tapping into her thoughts how frustrated she was the intense release faded quickly. There hadn't been any emotional component to her orgasm, and for a woman with a heart as big as Charlotte's, that left a gaping hole in the experience. Austin sensed her withdrawal immediately. He'd removed the balls while her mind had been lost in an orgasm she hadn't enjoyed.

"I'm sorry, Little Star." She took a step back but wouldn't look him in the eye. Fuck, he'd wanted to push her boundaries, but he damn well hadn't wanted to make her feel like a failure when it didn't work out. She nodded but kept her eyes downcast. When he reached up to lift her chin, she stepped back again, this time so quickly, she stumbled. Recovering before he could grab her, Charlotte muttered something about needing to freshen up before joining the others. Deciding she needed a chance to gather her thoughts, Austin didn't protest when she darted inside.

"That could have gone better, big brother." Austin recognized his brother's voice—hell, most of the planet recognized Kensington Adler's voice. As one of Hollywood's biggest names, Kensington had been on the sexiest man alive list the last several years—a distinction he could not have cared less about.

While most actors were busy making sure they were invited to all the right parties, so they could be photographed talking to the power-players, Kenz was behind the scenes, making the world a better place. His lawyers and family were the only ones who knew about his charitable foundation promoting literacy.

Kensington had struggled with reading as a kid—it still took him longer than most to read a page of text, but he'd never let any of that stand in his way, and Austin was damned proud of him. Taking a deep breath, Austin turned to face the man casually leaning against a vine-covered arbor.

"Glad you made it—even if your timing sucks."

"I'd say my timing is perfect. Hell, it's not every day I get to see the great Austin Adler fuck up so badly, his mate runs away to lick her wounded pride." Kensington Adler might be Mr. Suave to the rest of the world, but to his family, he never backed down from calling it exactly as he saw it. Giving an internal eye-roll, Austin admitted brutal honesty was likely a family trait. *Fucking hell.*

"Now, the way I see it, big brother, you're caught between a rock and a hard place. If you back off and treat your lovely mate as if she's made of spun glass, she's going to believe you don't think she can make it as your submissive. On the other hand, if you hold this hard line, she's going to know she's in way over her head. Either way, she's going to run."

Double fuck, he hadn't even considered she might try to leave the island.

Not wanting to depend on their telepathic connection, Austin pulled his phone from his pocket and quickly dialed Israel's number. Without saying hello, his brother answered on the first ring with a cryptic, "I'm already on it" before disconnecting. Israel was going to be pissed his earlier reminder to take things slow had been ignored, and he was left scrambling to contain the damage. Charlotte might not belong to Israel in the same way she did Austin, but there was no question, the middle Adler brother loved her in his own way.

"The girls are going to kick your ass. Hell, I may have to stay an extra day or two just to watch the show." Austin knew his brother was rubbing salt in his wounded ego.

It had taken some serious schedule juggling to get Kenz here at all. The movie he was wrapping up was being hailed as his biggest yet, and despite all the advance advertising, they were still shooting. Kensington had said it was going to take a huge miracle if they were going to meet the release date. Since Kensington was co-producing the action adventure, he had a lot on the line.

"Yeah, they are. Paris loves Charlotte already, and after she healed Cat..." Dragging his hand through his hair, Austin let his words trail off because just thinking about how Catalina was going to react made his balls want to head north and hide. When Kensington's brows shot up in surprise, Austin gave him a quick update on Cat's kidnapping and subsequent rescue. He gave his brother as much detail as he could about the injuries Catalina had sustained and how Charlotte had provided healing.

"Holy shit. Aren't you worried about every crackpot paramilitary group in the world trying to snatch her? Hell, I'm shocked our own government hasn't decided she needs to be in *protective custody* which translates to—we want her all to ourselves." Kensington's insight always surprised people who didn't know him well—he was so much more than the handsome movie star most people saw. Behind the pretty face was a brilliant business mind, and Kenz knew there was a job waiting for him at Adler Oil anytime he wanted it.

"I've got people checking it out, but I'm afraid you're right." They only had a few minutes before the wedding, so Austin led Kenz toward the villa's bar. After pouring them both a tumbler of Scotch, Austin settled on a stool at the other end of the bar from where Kensington sat, rolling the tumbler around on its edge. Neither of them said anything for long moments as Austin stared at the amber liquid.

"You're trying to keep all of this under wraps until after London's wedding, aren't you?" Kensington smiled as he shook his head. "Always trying to protect everyone. Damn, brother, we *are* all adults, you know. Hell, all of us are capable of sharing the spotlight—it comes from having nine siblings." Kensington shook his head and chuckled. "London will kick your ass if she finds out all this is going on, and everybody's walking on eggshells around her. Damn, give the girl a little credit, Austin."

"When did you get to be so fucking wise?"

"Humbling, isn't it?" Kensington's laughter helped Austin relax for the first time since Charlotte had run from him a half hour earlier. "Go check on your woman, and I'll see you at the wedding." Austin watched as Kenz strode away, knowing he was right. At some point, Austin was going to have to stop *parenting* his brothers and sisters, but it wasn't going to be easy—and it probably wasn't going to be today.

Chapter Seventeen

CHARLOTTE WIGGLED HER bare toes in the sand and let the residual warmth move through her. She loved the feeling of the earth's energy surging through her system like the beat of an ancient drum. Finding a place at the side of the wedding reception area, close to a wall of palms had been a blessing. She could still see the celebration, but she was far enough away to be somewhat forgotten—thank heavens. Austin's brothers and sisters had peppered her with polite questions, but Charlotte could have sworn they'd coordinated their efforts—none of the questions had been the same, and they'd had the strangest linear path.

She'd enjoyed the party until Austin started treating her like she was made of fucking porcelain. Damn it all to dapper dickheads, watching him act as though she was a dimwit made her want to scream. Israel must have sensed her frustration because he'd whisked his brother off a few minutes ago. She hadn't been able to hear their heated exchange over the music and laughter, but it was easy to see the two brothers disagreed about something... and Charlotte knew *she* was the *something* in question.

Growling under her breath, Charlotte was getting

damned tired of being coddled. It had been happening her entire life, and she was over it. Fucking hell, she'd hoped Austin would be different, that his dominant personality would push her limits rather than reinforcing them.

"I don't know what he did, but I'll help you kick his ass."

Spinning around, Charlotte was surprised to see London standing a few feet behind her. Gasping in surprise, Charlotte slapped her hand over her heart, trying to slow the erratic beating of her heart.

"Damn, I'm sorry. I didn't mean to frighten you." The beautiful bride had changed out of her wedding dress into a brightly colored sundress, showing off her golden tan.

"It's okay. I should have been paying attention, instead of staring off into space."

"Men will do that to do you sometimes… fry your brain, I mean. Sorry, I'm still trying to improve my communication skills." London giggled even as she shrugged her slender shoulders. Grasping London's forearm, to assure her there were no hard feelings, Charlotte squealed.

"Oh shit, I forgot about your gift." London pulled her back until they were almost hidden behind the palms. "We've only told my siblings and in-laws. Oh hell, who am I kidding, Paris can't keep a secret to save her, so it's probably already been published on every conceivable social media site."

"Oh, ye of little faith." Paris stepped into the small sheltered area and nudged her sister's shoulder. "I have only had time to brag on two sites, but I'll get to the others after you and your hotties take off for destinations unknown— well, unknown to you!" The youngest Adler's eyes danced with mischief. "I'll bet Charlotte knows if you're having twins or triplets. Heck, I'll bet she can tell you genders, too."

"Oh no, I... well, that's not... damn it." Charlotte had made this mistake once and had no plans to repeat it. The father had been furious that Charlotte and his excited wife had spoiled what he'd called the Great Goddess' to reveal. The young couple's marriage had suffered, and Charlotte had vowed to never reveal any maternity information unless the parents were on the same page.

"Don't look so stricken, you're scaring me." London grabbed her hand and laughed. "I can see you don't want to share without my husbands present, but don't think you're off the hook. Austin doesn't think I know what's going on, but he's wrong. All those years in college, kick-ass research, and hottie husbands and big brother still thinks I'm the helpless book nerd he had to defend from all the cool kids."

Charlotte wasn't fooled by London's blasé attitude, the bullied little girl her big brother defended still lurked inside the brilliant chemist and soon-to-be mama.

"We blame you for his hero complex, you know." Asia Adler stepped through the palms, her teasing smile settling on her younger sister. "He'd have told the rest of us to sink or swim."

"Give it up sisters, you all had a brother who looked out for you, I'm not buying a ticket for this guilt trip." London's teasing tone was emphasized by a hand resting on her hip in a saucy pose Charlotte suspected was well practiced.

All five Adler girls had slipped into the small space, and

Charlotte was amazed how at ease she felt with each of them despite having known them such a short time. Their easy camaraderie made her feel as though she was already a part of their family.

You are a part of their family, Charlotte.

Her mother's voice moved through her mind, startling her. Charlotte loved her mother, but this small assurance wasn't her usual M.O. No, Amaya Sumner's usual method of operation was more in line with the sink or swim mentality Asia mentioned earlier. Charlotte and her mom hadn't spent much time together after Amaya accepted a position on the Council of Magic.

Walk down the beach toward the pier, I'd like to see you, and I don't have much time. I have news about your grandfather, so I'd prefer you came alone.

"Charlotte, are you all right?" Asia Adler's question brought Charlotte back to the moment. Realizing the women were looking at her expectantly, she nodded.

"I'm sorry, I just remembered I was supposed to meet my mom down by the pier. She is only going to be on the island for a short time, and she won't be amused if I'm late." Asia, Brooklyn, and Catalina all frowned.

"Paris, why don't you make sure London finds her way back to her men, and we'll walk down to the pier with Charlotte."

Damn, her mom would be mad as an old wet hen if she showed up with three other women, and pissed off witches weren't anyone's idea of a good time.

"Listen, she asked me to come alone so she could talk to me about my granddad. My mom is perfectly charming as long as everything is going her way, but she won't be happy if I show up with an entourage." Asia was already looking over her shoulder, and Charlotte wasn't naïve, she knew Paris was probably already looking for Austin.

"Think about it, my mom, her sister, and grandfather are all on the Council… they can make life difficult in ways you can't even imagine. If you're going to follow me, please stay back far enough it won't be glaringly obvious you're shadowing me."

Without waiting for them to respond, Charlotte began walking quickly down the beach. Austin was probably going to be mad she'd left the party without telling him, but that was too bad. He'd already been nominated for asshat of the week, so he had the same clothes to get glad in as her grandmother always said. The closer she got to the pier, the more apprehensive she became.

When she and Austin had walked along the beach late last night, she'd asked what the bright lights were, and he'd told her it was the pier. But tonight, the area was shrouded in darkness, there was barely enough light from the one overhead light farther down the beach for her to make out the long wooden structure she knew extended well out into the water of a small bay. The closer she got to the pier, the more she regretted her decision to come alone. It wasn't like her mom to lead her into a dangerous situation.

Prior to mating with Austin, Charlotte had never been able to see particularly well at night, but tonight, she was able to make out three people standing against one of the concession buildings. Charlotte called out telepathically to her mom but didn't get a response. The hair on the back of her neck stood on end, and she felt the distinctive crackle of energy in the air around her, indicating there were magicals in the area, but she wasn't certain they were the men standing in front of her. Before she could turn around, she noted all three were men, and the man on the left was pointing a pistol at her, the other two were aiming their weapons behind her.

Charlotte's heart clenched when she realized she'd led Austin's sisters into a trap. The men were after her, but she worried they wouldn't hesitate to hurt anyone standing in their way.

"Come with us, Ms. Hays. If you don't resist, we will let your friends walk away unharmed." Charlotte didn't need to ask what would happen to the Adler sisters if she didn't cooperate.

"Where is my mother? What have you done with her?"

"One of the disadvantages of telepathic communication is the voice can be masked easily if there is enough outside stimulation—a wedding reception, for example." Not only were these men armed, but they were also so stupid, they were dangerous.

"Do you have any idea who you are dealing with? Imitating a member of the Council of Magic is a serious offense, but imitating my mother is a whole new level of stupid." For the first time in her life, Charlotte felt as though her mind was functioning on different levels. Having been taught to expect it, but knowing it was a part of the process didn't change the wonder she felt knowing her powers were finally being fully endowed.

Witches skills were continually refined, but like most magicals, their magic became exponentially stronger once they'd mated. Charlotte wiggled her toes deep into the warm sand. Dropping her hands to her sides and pressing the pads of her thumbs and middle fingers together, forming a circle, giving the power she was pulling from the earth a way to complete the cycle and build. The energy was beginning to vibrate at an ever-increasing frequency, and Charlotte felt her body begin to heat from the inside out.

Focusing her attention on the three men standing in front of her rather than their weapons kept her from becoming too distracted by fear. Anger was a more productive emotion, and she drew power from it as she considered what could happen to Asia, Brooklyn, and Catalina. Fucking hell, Cat had just been kidnapped, beaten, and traumatized. Charlotte had healed Cat's physical injuries but doubted anyone understood the depth of the young woman's emotional pain. Putting her in danger now was only going to exacerbate the problem.

Sending out a desperate telepathic call to anyone listening, Charlotte knew the key to getting through this was stalling. Her plea would be heard by any magical on the island and probably several nearby atolls as well. The best part was, the men standing a few feet from her couldn't hear her call for help. Magicals rarely used firearms, they didn't need to. There were plenty of other ways to deal with an enemy.

"Where are you planning to take me?"

"We have transportation waiting." The man on the left nodded toward the pier. "Let's go."

"Who sent you? Who do you work for?" Charlotte already suspected they were government funded, the question was... *which government?*

"Our bosses want to work with you. They asked me to assure you the arrangement will be mutually advantageous."

Yeah, right. I hope I don't look naïve enough to fall for that line.

Charley, we're watching from the trees. Your Aunt Gigi wants to turn them into some kind of rodent. Personally, I'm leaning toward staking them naked over a large ant hill near the Amazon.

There was no doubt in Charlotte's mind this time she really was hearing her mother. Amaya Sumner's droll sense of humor was one of her most endearing traits. What many people mistook for sarcasm was merely her mother's left-of-center way of looking at the world.

There is a virtual army surrounding you, Little Star. Your grandfather is going to magic a temporary shield between the soon-to-be-dead jerks standing in front of you and my sisters. When you see the flash of light, shimmer and run toward the trees on your right.

Hearing Austin's voice was such a relief, Charlotte felt her knees quiver and hoped they wouldn't fold out from under her. She could shimmer and disappear, but the men would still be able to see her footprints in the sand. If they'd done their homework, they'd still be able to nab her out from under everyone's nose.

Charlotte, I'm appalled you think the three stooges can best your beloved grandfather and his two brilliant daughters. Honestly, this is almost boring. I left a party in Madrid, and Papa was dancing with a contingent of bikini-clad beauties on a neighboring island, so let's get this done.

Her Aunt Gigi's voice was a balm to her soul. They'd always been extremely close and knowing her mother's only sister was here helped settle her nerves. Brigitte Stafford could go from droll amusement to demolition mode in the blink of an eye, and it sounded like she was already teetering toward destruction.

Before she had time to worry about how this was all going to play out, the world behind her seemed to explode in a brilliant blue/white ball of light she recognized as magic. Instinct took over, narrowing her focus to the task at hand. Before she'd completely shimmered out of sight, Charlotte let the men see her take several steps toward the water. She quickly doubled back, being sure to stay close enough to the wall of brilliant light, the glare would make it difficult for them to notice her footprints in the soft sand. She needn't have worried because the wind swirled around her like a tornado with her in the calm center.

Shielding her eyes from the flying sand, Charlotte saw two huge wolves emerge from the tree cover and run toward the men. They were beautiful… and huge. When she heard one of the majestic animals howl in pain, all thoughts of self-preservation evaporated into a fine mist as her anger raged out of control. Turning, Charlotte took two steps before she felt her body explode out of the dress she wore. Landing on all fours, she ran like the wind. In seconds, she'd tackled one of the men, biting his femur with such force she heard the bone snap.

Taking his gun in her teeth, she tossed the weapon out of his reach, then turned to the man taking aim at the wolf she recognized as her mate. Her eyesight was so much sharper, her sense of smell so acute, she could differentiate between her mate's blood and that of the others. Knowing the would-be kidnapper had hurt her mate enough to draw blood blocked all logic from her mind. Charlotte was acting on primal instinct alone.

She didn't think about her family standing nearby. She

didn't consider their individual magical abilities, nor did she take time to contemplate how powerful their combined talents would be. In the back of her mind, Charlotte heard a cacophony of voices shouting at her to run, but leaving Austin alone with a man intent of separating them wasn't an option. Israel had one man pinned to the ground, and she had the other backed up against a concession stand, advertising a multitude of meat offerings—the irony wasn't lost on her.

Charlotte felt herself being lifted into the air and moved to the edge of the trees where her mother and aunt stood waiting. By the time her feet touched the ground, she'd shifted back into human form. With a twirl of her finger, Charlotte's Aunt Gigi covered her nude body with a dress exactly like the one she'd ruined a few minutes earlier. Her mother's eyes widened when she took in Charlotte's disheveled hair and dirt smudged arms. Shaking her head, she absently waved her hand, and Charlotte felt a familiar tingling move in a slow sweep over her from the tips of her toes all the way up to the top of her head. She didn't need a mirror to know she now looked as though she'd just stepped from the pages of a fashion magazine.

A swirl of gray smoke encircled the man who'd hurt Austin, and in seconds, the man threatening her mate was bound, shoulders to feet, with thick rope. Charlotte watched her grandfather grin, assuming he was pleased with himself for a job well done. Following his gaze more closely, she realized her grandfather was watching Cooper pry the gun from Catalina's fingers as the other woman cursed like a sailor. Asia stepped up behind Cat, slipping another small pistol into the waistband of her pants and the small of her back.

"Give the gun to Cooper, Catalina. You know how men get if you don't let them play with the toys that go bang."

Charlotte was torn between worry for the two women and longing to have sisters who would have her back like the Adler siblings. What would it be like to have sisters who loved you enough to put themselves in danger to back you up?

To the side, Sheriff Trinity Stone was holding back a spitting-mad Paris.

"Let me go, you big oaf, my sisters need help. I'll tie that asshat up, so it'll take hedge trimmers to get him out of the bindings."

"First of all, your sisters do not need your help, they are doing just fine. And you don't need to be involved when Cooper discovers that little exchange that just took place behind Catalina's back." Shaking his head as the rope began wrapping around the second man, the sheriff grinned. "Damn, I'm anxious to find out why that coil of rope never seems to end." She pulled against the hand he had wrapped around her upper arm, but it was wasted effort. "I'm going to paddle your ass for taking off after I told you to stay with London. She's pregnant for heaven's sake, she needs to stay calm and be protected."

Paris pointed to the side where London stood, bouncing on the balls of her feet in obvious excitement between her two husbands. Her sister's excited voiced carried across the distance.

"Damn, we had the most exhilarating wedding ever. Didn't I tell you my siblings were fun? Holy hell, this is going to be a great story to tell our grandchildren. You said you'd give me an amazing wedding, and you were right."

Paris didn't remember ever seeing her studious sister this excited.

"You mean that London? The one everyone's been trying to protect, so she doesn't feel her big day is being eclipsed by everything going on around her? *That London?*" Paris didn't even try to keep the sarcasm out of her voice.

"Still turning you over my knee and paddling your bare ass. When I tell you to stay put, I damn well mean it. You put yourself in danger, and that's not acceptable, you little hellion. And don't think for a minute I won't be watching you while you're staying with your sister." Paris's glare would have withered the balls off most men, but the Sheriff just shook his head. "Not going to work, brat."

Charlotte stared as the two disappeared into the trees. Paris was cursing a blue streak before Charlotte heard what sounded like a hand striking bare flesh.

"You want to start this here within earshot of your family or take it back to our suite?" Trinity's growled words were the last thing Charlotte heard from the pair as they disappeared from view.

The stress of the past hour finally caught up with her, and Charlotte burst out in hysterical laughter.

"Oh Goddess, this isn't good."

Her mother's words came from somewhere in the distance, but Charlotte didn't care. Trinity and Paris's bickering had given her an outlet for the glut of emotion— laughing was so much better than crying, and she worried the tears were going to fall soon enough.

Chapter Eighteen

AUSTIN LISTENED AS Amaya Sumner explained how the three men had lured Charlotte away from the party. She hadn't been the one to put out the call, but she'd picked up the echoes since the magical they'd used to communicate telepathically was a woman Amaya had dealt with before. The young woman had betrayed her gift and would face sanctions from the Council before being forced to undergo a lengthy refresher in magical ethics.

"I'll deal with her, Amaya, you're too emotionally invested to be *fair*."

Austin fought to contain his smile when Audric and Amaya turned in synch to stare at Brigitte who shrugged nonchalantly. The woman he knew as Mistress B wasn't fooling anyone with her faux look of innocence, but then he was quite certain she wasn't trying too hard.

"I swear she is going to be struck by lightning someday for uttering such outrageous nonsense." Turning to Asia, the elderly man transformed before their eyes into what Austin suspected Charlotte's grandfather looked like as a much younger man.

"Honey, you and your sisters did a fine job of guarding those scoundrels while we tied them up. You should ditch that Italian fellow you're sweet on and come to the party in Rio with me. Carnival is always more fun with a hot girl on my arm."

The man was a flirt of the first order. He knew perfectly well Asia wasn't going to go, but he'd distracted everyone long enough for his daughters to cast spells on the bound men. The one with the broken leg was no longer howling in pain as he slumped forward in what looked like a drugged stupor. In the blink of an eye, they were gone as was all evidence they'd ever been there.

"What did you do with them?" Austin wasn't surprised Catalina was the first to ask what they were all wondering. "I wanted to ask them a few questions. Okay, a lot of questions. And I was looking forward to knocking them around a little as well."

"Stand in line, little sister, questions are my forte." Asia flashed a brilliant smile in Audric's direction, and Austin was shocked when the man burst out laughing.

"Asia, if you ever decide to broaden your horizons, the Council of Magic would hire you in a heartbeat. When your powers are fully manifested, you're going to be unstoppable." Shaking his head, he swirled his fingers in front of her, then held out the golden cards that materialized in his palm. "Give one of these to each of your brothers and sisters, dear. Not only is Charlotte now a part of your family, but all of you are also a part of ours. Should you ever find yourself in a pickle, this card is all you need to call us to your side."

Asia fanned the cards like a world-class poker player, looking bewildered. "These cards are blank."

"Yes, dear, they are." Turning his attention to his

daughters, Audric smiled. "You two have prisoners to deal with. I'll expect a full report by morning. I want to know who sent them and why. Wipe their memories once you're finished—I'll leave it to your discretion how far back to go, but it's probably best not to go back to grammar school." His pointed look at his youngest daughter brought another negligent shrug.

"I'll call in markers in Washington and put a stop to this nonsense. If we'd wanted to share Charlotte, we'd have done so years ago. I swear, the whole world is going to hell in a handbasket." In the time it took Austin to blink, the man was gone. No theatrics this time—just *gone*.

"Personally, I hate it when he does that, but you get used to it." Gigi turned to look up the beach.

Kensington, Bronx, and Cleveland were walking Charlotte back to the resort where he could see Evander waiting, muscular arms crossed over his chest. No doubt his friend was pissed and felt guilty about the threat to one of his guests. The security at the resort was top-notch, but nothing could have prevented this mess, but unavoidable wouldn't matter to Evander. He would not be pleased Charlotte had been endangered on his watch. Austin returned his attention to the small group gathered nearby.

"Thanks for the clothes, I wasn't looking forward to walking around in my birthday suit." Israel gave Amaya a smile that looked almost humble. Austin fought the urge to roll his eyes, and Gigi snorted a laugh. "Where did you send the perps? I'd like to ask them a few questions, and I'm sure Cameron Barnes would appreciate being consulted as well."

"Aww, the illustrious Cameron Barnes. The only thing

more mythical than a retired witch is a retired special agent." Austin didn't even try to hide his amusement this time because Amaya was dead on.

Everyone knew Cam was no more retired than Kent and Kyle West—the former Navy SEALs' special forces team had an impressive record as a contract agency willing to take missions others swore couldn't be accomplished.

"The men are being held in a secure section at the Council of Magic headquarters. They'll be healthy, happy, and thoroughly muddled before being returned to their employer."

Austin had never had the opportunity to visit the facility, hell, he wasn't even sure where it was. Everything he'd read indicated the headquarters was hidden in plain sight with portals around the world. Something niggled at the back of his mind, but it didn't have time to gel, so he let it go. Right now, his mate needed him, and he didn't want to wait any longer than absolutely necessary to make his way back to her.

Austin was amazed at how protective he'd become in the short time since they'd mated. He finally understood why his father had always made his wife a priority—the man had ten children, but there was never any doubt who held his heart. Amaya studied him for so long he was becoming uncomfortable. The intensity of her gaze made him feel as though she was looking into his soul.

"Your mother is right, you are the perfect mate for my daughter."

Austin blinked in disbelief. Hell, her words shocked him in more ways than one. His surprise must have shown because she waved him off with an easy smile.

"The veil between this realm and the beyond isn't impenetrable, Austin. Most people shy away from the hereafter because it's an unknown. If you open your heart, the veil becomes transparent, and once you glimpse the splendor of the other side, it's not frightening at all." Stunned didn't begin to describe his feeling.

"You've talked to my mom? Recently? Since the accident?" He wasn't sure how he felt about her revelation. One part of him was thrilled to know his mom approved of his mating with Charlotte, but there was another part of him that was wildly envious Amaya could talk to the woman whose voice he'd longed to hear since she was taken from them far too soon. Warm fingers caressed his cheek, and Austin realized Amaya was standing in front of him, compassion reflecting in her deep emerald eyes.

"Yes, I've talked to her. Your dad has spoken to members of the council on several occasions. Your parents are both lovely, and I'm grateful to be one of those watching over you and your siblings in their stead."

Austin took a deep breath, trying to ease his rioting emotions. The warmth in her expression eased the tension, and he was finally able to draw in a deep breath.

"Go. We'll talk more about this later." The last thing he saw was a wave of her hand before he found himself lost in a swirl of brilliant color. "Charlotte needs you." Amaya's voice was a distant echo fading as he realized he was now standing outside the villa he shared with his mate and brother. Within seconds, Evander appeared at his side, looking formidable, but his friend didn't look at all confused.

"Neat trick. Don't suppose you'd like to introduce me

to the hot redhead—the one wearing the fuck me black leather boots, not the one who zapped you a half mile with the flick of her wrist." Evander's voice held equal parts amusement and caution which made Austin smile.

"Brigitte Stafford—the hot redhead—is not a woman to be trifled with, my friend. She is a powerful member of the Council of Magic. Her name means light, and she's more than earned the moniker, one of the brightest women I've ever met. Ms. Stafford is also a Domme, so unless you're anxious to have your balls caged and weights tied to the end of your dick, you might want to rethink the context of your interest." To his credit, Evander didn't respond other than to laugh.

"Your family sure knows how to throw a party. Although I have to admit, things did get a lot more interesting when your in-laws showed up." Evander's grin made him look far younger than the intimidating man who'd been standing like a sentinel beside the resort a few minutes earlier.

"I can smell you all over her, so I know you've already claimed Charlotte—when you get ready to make it legal, I'd love to host the event. I promise to keep everyone as safe as possible."

"Fuck, you have to be kidding." Austin couldn't hold back his laughter, despite the thread of remorse he heard in his friend's voice. Hell, after the way they'd turned the resort upside down tonight, he owed his friend at least that much. "There wasn't a damned thing you could have done to prevent what happened tonight. Those assholes barely stepped foot on the island, so I'd say your reputation for security is firmly in place. And London is thrilled to have had an adventure wedding—whatever the hell that is." Evander's lips quirked and his nod was so slight, Austin might have missed the small acknowledgment if he hadn't been watching his friend closely.

"As soon as we set a date, I'll be in touch. Take my brothers a bottle of your best whiskey and add it to my tab. I appreciate them escorting Charlotte back here, and you'll feel better if you spend some time listening to them recount what real Adler disasters look like."

"I'll do that, and I'll enjoy sharing that very expensive bottle with them since I'm off duty for the rest of the night." Evander's expression softened as his eyes darted briefly down the villa's hallway. "Now, that I know you've calmed down, I'll leave you to care for your sweet woman. Don't be too hard on her. Sometimes, people do the wrong thing for the right reason."

Austin let his own gaze move to the darkened hall before returning to his friend, but the man hadn't given him a chance to respond—he was already gone. *Damned Special Forces guys always move like fucking ghosts.*

"I APPRECIATE YOUR call, Brigitte. I've discovered it's wise to keep my eyes and ears open when it comes to the machinations of what the hidden hands of the agency are up to. The video of your interrogation was enlightening." Cam Barnes leaned back in his supple leather chair, watching the monitor in front of him, listening to the beautiful witch he'd known since she joined his club years earlier. Her knowing smile made him chuckle—watching the magical

Mistress B and her sister question the men sent to kidnap Charlotte was as entertaining as it was educational.

"It really wasn't much of a challenge, the agency is seriously slacking, Cam. When did they stop training their recruits to control their physiological responses during interrogation? Those guys heart rates were all over the place, their respiration rates spiked before we even got started. I swear I thought the youngest was going to cry when I dangled a cock cage in front of his very sad little penis, and the older one got a hard-on... Goddess, I'd love to tie him to a St. Andrew's Cross." Cam could ordinarily hide his emotions, but he leaned his head back and barked out his laughter.

"You are ruthless, Brigitte." It was true. It was also one of the many things they had in common. He'd also been merciless when questioning suspects, but he hadn't had the added advantage of magic—*damn it*. There was a part of him that wished like hell he had even a fraction of the young witch's magical ability.

"Just one of the many reasons everyone loves me." Brigitte's voice was eclipsed by the excited laughter of his children filling the room as the door of his home office swung open. For a Master known for his strict enforcement of protocol in his club, Cam was ridiculously slack where his children were concerned. Perhaps it was because he knew with all the risks he'd taken as a younger man... hell, he was lucky he'd lived long enough to find the love of his life, let alone become a father.

"We'll talk again soon. I'll be in Texas next week. In the meantime, remind your children witchy friends are the best friends."

Watching her wave her hands in front of her, smoke trailing in her slender fingers' wake before the screen went blank, Cam suddenly realized the smoke was all too real. *What the fuck?*

"Wow, Dad. Cool special effects." His daughter, Chloe, grinned as she waved away the pale blue smoke. Chloe had gotten the best of her both parents. She was beautiful, brilliant, and had a take no prisoners attitude Cam both loved and hated. Whereas his son, Phillip, clearly took after his biological father. Tall for his age, the blonde-haired, blue-eyed boy was already solving puzzles most adults walked away from in frustration.

"Is that for me?" Phillip's excited voice could only mean one thing. Turning, Cam wanted to groan when he saw what had to be the biggest Erector set he'd ever seen. Damn, Phillip would probably build a fleet of robots with that set.

"Dad, is this mine? Holy crap-a-molie. This laptop isn't even available in stores yet." Chloe looked at him as if he'd personally hung the moon and stars before laughing and launching herself into his arms. "You are the best dad ever."

He wasn't fooled by her adoration, knowing all too well how fleeting it could be. More than once, his sweet first-born had tried to play her dads off one another—it never ended well for her, but he knew she hadn't finished trying.

"As much as I'd enjoy taking credit for the wonderful gifts, you can both thank Miss Brigitte when you see her at the picnic next week." The Wests hosted a huge picnic every year, one of the events club members and their families looked forward to. Kent and Kyle's wife, Tobi, started the event with the help of their mother, Lilly, and it had quickly become a member favorite.

Settling back in his chair after the kids left with their gifts, Cam turned to look out over their enormous back-yard. He loved the openness between their palatial home and the river—any intruder would be spotted by their security team before they finished stepping out of the water. The front and sides were lined with a seven-foot high fence with pulsing electrical charges that put the local farms and ranches fences to shame. The security feature hadn't been cheap, but E.G.A. Fabrication in nearby Sealy had built a solid steel fence that looked stately and formi-dable. Feeling her presence, Cam turned to see the love of his life standing in the open door.

Dr. Cecelia Barnes was one of the most sought-after pediatric surgeons in the world. Techniques she'd devel-oped were now the standard in every children's hospital. Brilliant with the face of an angel and a body made for sin. Damn, the woman was fucking perfect. Shifting his gaze over her shoulder, Cam gave Carl a quick nod, then smiled when the only man he'd ever loved reached around the wife they shared to pull her flush against his bare chest.

"I just finished my shower—it appears I'm ahead of you two." Dressed in nothing but a low-slung pair of faded jeans, frayed along the hem framing sun-kissed feet, the man could still kick up Cam's heart rate after all these years.

"I need to make a couple of calls, and since I took my shower an hour ago, why don't you get our lovely wife settled in a bubble bath? When you return, I'll update you on a situation I've been monitoring for a couple of weeks. I think you'll find it interesting." Carl's brow quirked in question, but he didn't ask.

Cam hadn't made any secret of wanting to interview Charlotte about her ability to disappear in a cloud of glitter—fuck, that had to be one of the most amazing things he'd seen in a long time. Despite knowing Brigitte for years, he'd never seen her perform any magic other than making men worship her and expensive gifts for his children appearing out of thin air. It was damned humbling to admit he had missed the connection between Brigitte and Charlotte, but since he'd handed over many of the day-to-day operations of Dark Desires, he didn't always see member applications or the results of their background checks unless there was an obvious problem.

"Okay, what's so damned important I had to leave the most beautiful woman in the world alone in a tub designed for three?"

Cam turned, surprised to see Carl already seated in one of the two leather wingback chairs facing his desk. Hell, he couldn't believe he'd been so lost in thought, he hadn't heard the other man enter the room.

"Damn, Cam, it's unlike you to be so distracted. What's up?" Halfway through his summary of the call from Brigitte, Carl waved him to a stop.

"You're telling me Charlotte Hays can heal people by taking on their injuries, then healing herself at an accelerated rate?" Cam nodded, knowing where the other man was headed. "And you're hung up on the fact she can fucking disappear in a sparkly cloud?" When Cam nodded again, Carl shook his head. "I'm sure you have some sort of reason, but I'll be damned if I can figure it out."

Carl, a retired Navy SEAL, had a unique understanding of what was valuable in the field. He was no stranger to covert military sanctioned *and unsanctioned* operations, but Cam could see Carl had no idea what Cam saw in Charlotte's ability to disappear.

"I think the ability to disappear is the tip of the iceberg with Charlotte. Call it gut instinct, but I know there is so much more. Healing is not new, magicals have been able to heal in a variety of ways since before recorded history, but I'm telling you the Agency isn't as interested in healing as they are in prevention. Having an agent or contact who can insert themselves covertly into a situation, gather the intel, and get out without being detected is the pot of gold at the end of the rainbow."

Cam could tell by the look on Carl's face he wasn't convinced, but it didn't matter—time was certainly on his side. For now, he'd put out some fires at the agency. The power players weren't happy their operators had been dropped at their front door with no indication of how they'd gotten there. The multiple hoops a person had to jump through before being allowed to enter the secured perimeter intimidated most visitors. And if electrified razor wire and armed guards didn't turn away unwanted guests, they were quickly identified with the wide range of monitoring equipment covering every inch of the grounds and facility.

To say the agents were having a hard time explaining how they appeared between one camera frame and the next was the fucking understatement of the year. Showing up on the curb of one of the most secure facilities in the world without any explanation as to how you got there tended to toss a lot of red flags in the air. Cam managed to throw them off Charlotte's trail by assuring them she was still on the island with Austin, but he didn't expect them to be dissuaded for long. Knowing about her magical abilities was the reason they'd sent three agents to bring her in, but having the men returned to them with no memory of anything after the office Christmas party two years ago was a big hurdle for the Agent in Charge to get over. Cam shook his head and chuckled as he related everything to Carl who was laughing out loud by the time he finished.

"Damn, I wish I could have been a fly on the wall when those agents tried to explain their sudden appearance. You have to give Amaya and Brigitte credit for making fools of Spies-R-Us. Damn, I'm going to buy Mistress B a drink."

"Speaking of drinks, I could use one." Their wife strode confidently into the room, wearing the sheerest negligée Cam had ever seen. This was Dr. Cecelia Barnes, not the submissive Cam and Carl enjoyed tying to their bed and playing with for hours on end. This was a woman who was tired of waiting on the men who'd promised to join her. *This woman was a force to be reckoned with*—and he looked forward to the challenge.

Chapter Nineteen

PARIS STARED OUT the floor to ceiling windows, lost in the memory of her last few days at the resort before returning to her sister's home. The night three men tried to kidnap her future sister-in-law, the excitement hadn't ended on the beach where Charlotte's family had shown up in force. The real excitement had followed her all the way back to the villa she'd shared with Sheriff Trinity Stone. Sighing to herself, Paris tried to refocus her thoughts on what she'd witnessed that night and away from the wild evening's second feature.

Watching Audric, Amaya, and Brigitte's magic was an eye-opening experience even for a woman who knew her brothers were shifters. How cool would it be to be able to tie people up with magic, then send them to who knows where with just a flick of your wrist? Leaning her forehead against the cool glass, Paris let out a breath she didn't realize she'd been holding. A sliver of moonlight peaked from between the clouds, casting sparkling diamonds of light dancing over the smooth surface of the swimming pool.

Paris loved what her brothers-in-law called the court-yard. The enclosed space was surrounded on two sides by

Eli's medical clinic, and on the other sides, the well-landscaped space was bordered by the home Eli had occupied before he and his brother, Evan, married London. Slipping out the door, Paris padded on bare feet to the water's edge. Dragging her toes through the water, she sighed.

"Maybe a swim will help me sleep." If her body was exhausted, maybe her mind would shut down long enough for her to get a few hours rest. She hadn't seen Sheriff Stone since returning to the small town outside of Boston where he was the lead law enforcement officer. Paris was fascinated with the small enclave that was the hub for Eli and Evan's pack. Dark clouds floated over the moon, shrouding the pool area in darkness, fairy lights along the curved edges of the well-manicured lawn and underwater lights the only sources of illumination. The ambiance was more temptation than Paris could resist.

TRINITY STONE STOOD in the shadows, watching the play of emotions on Paris Adler's face as she stared out the window. He'd stayed away for a week, but tonight, he'd sworn he could feel her loneliness. The pull was more than he could resist. Alerting the Monroe's security team he was headed their way had been a mere formality, his cousins had always given him unlimited access to the medical facility compound. Watching the petite hellion he couldn't get out of his head walk to the edge of the water, he heard her whisper about a swim helping her sleep a heartbeat before the sundress she wore was floating to the stone apron surrounding the pool.

It was only a heartbeat or two before she dove smoothly into the water, but every detail of the picture of her standing naked at the pool's edge was forever etched in his mind. The pale lights along the shrubbery were just enough to illuminate the luscious curves of her ass cheeks—ivory mounds he'd had in his hands just a few days earlier. At her front, the underwater lights highlighted taut nipples begging to be sucked into ever-tightening peaks.

Realizing he was behaving like a damned peeping Tom, Trin stepped from the shadows. Moving closer to the pool, he stood with his feet apart, arms crossed over his chest, watching Paris skim the top of the water with smooth strokes. He found himself mesmerized by her nearly perfect form. How many hours had she spent in the water to make it look so natural? As a shifter, Trinity was an excellent swimmer, but he'd never put any effort into making it look effortless. The realization she'd spent the past few years in California made him frown. Damn, how often had that perfect body been on display in some obscene bikini for a bunch of horny frat-rats to ogle?

Paris continued to swim, but he knew she'd sensed his presence—the brat was deliberately snubbing him. *Not a wise move, minx. You can't ignore me forever, and I'm expending a lot less energy than you are.*

AUSTIN WAS ALERTED when Charlotte entered the penthouse elevator. Preparing for the coming storm, he smiled to himself, wondering what she was going to be more unhappy about—the fact he'd turned off the alarm and left her sleeping peacefully in their bed or her empty desk.

He'd opened his office door enough to hear what was taking place on the other side and smiled when he heard the familiar squeak of her chair. Mentally counting the seconds, he wasn't disappointed when her surprised gasp sounded in less than five seconds. Stomping into his office, she stared at him for long moments before demanding to know why her desk had been cleaned out. Austin moved purposefully to the door, closing it softly before engaging the lock with a snick that seemed so much louder in the tense silence surrounding them.

"Charlotte, I told you what would happen if we worked in the same office." He let his gaze move over her bare legs, lightly tanned after their time on the beach. Austin heard her soft intake of air as he let his eyes move up to the short sundress he'd left on the bed with instructions for her to wear it and nothing else.

"Do you have on panties?" He saw her eyes widen and knew the truth before she slowly nodded. "Oh baby, I warned you about the penalty for disobedience." Pulling a wide wooden ruler from his top desk drawer, Austin moved to stand in front of her. "Give me the panties, Charlotte." Her eyes widened before narrowing in challenge. "Every second you delay adds to your punishment."

"I came in here for answers, not to satisfy your kinky need to see my bare ass." Austin didn't respond but let his eyes flicker toward the large clock on the wall. Rolling her eyes, she reached under her dress, pulling the offending garment down her sharply legs before scooping them off the floor to place them in his outstretched hand.

"I want to know why you fired me."

He froze. Her barely whispered words shocking him. Damn it all to hell, they'd talked about this. Didn't she think he was serious when he'd said he wanted her to return to school? Austin knew it was her dream and wanted to do everything he could to help her realize it.

"Bend over the desk, my lovely, disobedient mate. I'm going to remind you why it's not wise to ignore my instructions." With her bent over the edge of his desk, he smoothed his palm from the small of her back, tracing a path over the globes of her sweet ass before bunching the back of her dress in his fist, drawing it up to her waist. "I do so love looking at your bare ass, baby." Three quick strikes, leaving three bright red stripes, had her gasping before he heard the first sob. Lifting her into his arms, Austin moved to the sofa at the other side of the room.

"This isn't the way I wanted our morning to go, Charlotte. I had other plans for you—including being bent over the desk for an entirely different purpose." She was still sniffling, her tears soaking through his shirt, making him grateful his apartment was only a short elevator ride away.

"Why? Why do I have to leave? Just because you claimed me? How is that fair?" The disappointment in her voice tested his resolve, but in the end, he knew they couldn't work in such close proximity.

"I was serious when I said you are already enrolled in school. If you are sitting outside my office, I'll never get anything done." It was the truth; his cock was already ready to burst from his trousers. If he didn't get inside her soon, there wasn't going to be enough blood left to keep his brain functioning. Lifting her enough to open his pants, Austin freed himself from their confines. Slipping his fingers through her folds, he smiled.

"So wet for me already, I think someone liked their spanking more than she wants to admit. Sink down on me, mate. Take me inside your hot pussy. I'll let you have the reins for sixty seconds—I suggest you make them count." Charlotte sank down on him in a move so quick, he felt as though the top of his head was going to blow off.

"Damn, that feels so good. I love the way you stretch me, that delicious burn as my pussy struggles to accommodate your big cock."

Fuck! As if her body wasn't enough to shred his control, her words were going to push him over the edge before her damned minute was up.

"Your shaft is so hot, I can feel every bump and ridge searing me as you push between my swollen tissues." She rocked forward, changing the angle just enough to let the hard ridge surrounding his cock head skim her G-spot. "Feel that? My body is already starting to tremble. I can feel myself creaming for you." She'd barely gotten the last few words out when he felt her liquify around him. Charlotte leaned her head back, a soft cry leaving her lips as she shattered in his arms.

Grinding his teeth to hold off his own release, Austin tried every trick he'd learned as a Dom to control his own pleasure, but in the end, it wasn't enough. Charlotte's whispered "I love you, Master" sent him spiraling over the edge. Holding her down as he pulsed seed against her cervix, Austin's imagination kicked into high gear as he wondered what their future children would look like. He'd never considered having a family, but now he couldn't imagine a life without a house filled to the brim with kids.

Pulling his limp mate against his chest, Austin pressed his palm against her back, drawing lazy circles over her tanned skin. He'd insisted if she wanted to sunbathe, it had to be done in the nude in a variety of exhibitionist poses. It had been the stuff of erotic fantasies, and Austin was grateful for his insight now because he definitely appreciated the lack of tan lines. He was overwhelmed with a sense of contentment when he felt Charlotte snuggle closer.

"I only had two semesters left when I quit to work full-time, hopefully, that hasn't changed too much." He wasn't going to spoil the surprise by telling her that he'd lobbied for her to gain credit for her experience at Adler Oil so she could easily finish in one semester.

Taking a deep breath, Austin went still at the change he detected in her scent. Burying his face in her hair to sniff the tender skin below her ear, he smiled to himself. It seemed they'd be starting their family sooner than he'd planned.

"Oh, Goddess, Austin, I'm not sure I can go another round with you." He wanted to laugh out loud because she'd just fucked him into a coma. Hell, she was giving him way too much credit if she thought he could recover that quickly. "There is a small part of me that's glad I don't have to work today—I'm really tired. I hope I'm not coming down with something."

Oh yeah, you're definitely going to be dealing with something, my lovely mate.

"Your classes start next week. Until then, I want you to start planning our wedding." He'd proposed to her their last night at the resort. Evander managed to fill their pool outside their villa with floating containers of floral arrangements with candles ringing the pool's raised edge. Austin had seen tears in Charlotte's eyes when she'd stepped onto the terrace and knew how grateful she'd been for his friend's effort.

They'd eaten a wonderful candlelit dinner before he'd gotten down on one knee to propose. Being able to have the platinum, two-carat, princess-cut diamond ring flown to the island was one of the few times Austin could remember being truly thankful for the wealth he'd accumulated.

Charlotte pulled back, sitting up she met his amused grin, tilting her head to the side as if she was trying to figure out a puzzle.

"Are you in a rush, lover? Afraid some frat rat will steal my heart?" A surge of heat moved through him so fast, he wondered if he would spontaneously combust. Shaking her head, Charlotte gave him a rueful smile. "I cannot believe you took me seriously, Master. You know you are the only man who will ever own my heart. As much as I enjoy it when you choose to invite Israel into our bed, I will never love him the way I do you."

"Charlotte, I love you more than life itself. Any man touching you without my express permission is going to lose his hand." He hoped his smile took some of the threat out of his words, but from her raised brows, Austin was sure he hadn't been successful. "How long will it take you to plan the wedding?"

"You seem to be in a hurry all the sudden."

Charlotte studied him so closely, he started to wonder if she'd taken lessons from his sister, London, who looked at everything like the researcher she was. Hell, worse yet, Charlotte was emulating Asia who was a shark attorney in anyone's view.

"Wait a minute. You weren't snuggling with me a minute ago... you smelled me. Did I smell different to you? Because London told me Eli and Evan knew she was pregnant long before she suspected because they said she smelled different."

"Doesn't it figure I'd mate with a woman every bit as brilliant as my sisters? Damn, there will be no secrets from you, will there? Yes, you smell different, and in case there is any question in your mind, I'm thrilled. I was looking forward to becoming an uncle, but being a father is going to be even better." He'd thoroughly debased her earlier, and he was damned proud of that fact. Smoothing back a lock of her hair that had escaped the bun she typically wore to work, Austin caressed the side of her face.

"Give me a date, baby? Something under six weeks."

The words had barely left his lips when a piece of parchment floated down from above them. The paper seemed to have materialized out of thin air, and he suddenly realized how interesting it was going to be having wizards and witches as in-laws. Charlotte grabbed the paper, holding it up so they could both read the fanciful script.

Charlotte...

Elope, then host a big party.

Weddings are o errated.

our parents are enjoying another extended honeymoon.

our grandfather is in Egypt... Don't ask.

I'm closer, but weddings gi e me hi es.

Congrats to me on becoming a Great Aunt!

Gigi

CHARLOTTE STARED AT the parchment note, and Austin's heart ached at the lost look in her eyes. Hell, she didn't know whether to laugh or cry.

How is it possible all the people who are important to me are too busy to help me plan or attend my wedding? She hadn't asked the question aloud but was certain he'd heard her just the same. Shaking her head, she let her gaze move to the floor. *Damn. I hate seeing that look of sympathy. I've seen it in people's eyes all my life where my family is concerned.*

"Don't. Please." When she tried to stand, he tightened his hold, sliding his hand around the back of her neck, massaging the tense muscles before moving his fingers along the underside of her chin, lifting it until her eyes met his.

"Your family cannot steal your joy unless you allow it." He heard the soft snick of a latch closing and knew Israel had entered through a side door most people didn't know existed. When she started to divert her attention to his brother, he held her chin with his fingers. "No, baby. Eyes on me. I want you to listen to what Israel has to say. I suspect he's been making calls and has news for us." With five sisters, Austin saw the slight quiver of her chin and knew how close she was to a meltdown—damn, he wanted to kick her family's collective asses for casting a shadow over this moment.

"Charlotte, did you know Kensington is in town?" She seemed surprised by Israel's question, but Austin knew exactly what his brother was leading up to. "He's on his way over now, and well, sorry if I stole some of your thunder, but I told him about you and Austin getting married. Kensington has fans all over this damned city, and he's determined to take you shopping for a dress today."

"Why? He barely knows me." Austin knew her question was part tinged with hope, so he was going to hold his comment and let Israel take the lead.

"Are you kidding? You *are* family, sweetheart, and for a straight guy who has a small army dressing him, my brother has great taste." Israel gave her a wicked grin before leaning down to pick up her dress from the floor. Raising a brow, he held out his hand to Austin. "She can't try on wedding dresses without panties. You know how pushy those sales ladies are—they won't stay out of the dressing room and gossip worse than the subs at the club." They'd barely gotten Charlotte dressed and her hair back in place when the door of his office opened, and Kensington stalked inside.

"What's with Broom Hilda at the reception desk? She not getting laid or what?" Casting a million-dollar smile at Charlotte, Kensington pulled her into a big hug. "I'm so glad Austin found you, I hope I can find someone as amazing as you. Hell, if you decided you…" Austin's growl from behind her cut Kensington off, making him wince. "Okay, well, let's not go there. Damn, big brother, you're awfully cranky for a guy who's mated a woman who is equally brilliant and beautiful."

"Good save, little brother. Hollywood hasn't stolen all your tact, thank Goddess." Austin pulled her out of Kensington's hold and into his own. "Have fun shopping, Charlotte. I'm going to make a few calls. You find a dress you love, and I'll do the rest." They'd be married within a week if he could pull it together.

"I'll help him, Charlotte… so he doesn't do anything crazy like pick out lime green and hot pink decorations." Asia strode into the room, her signature sky-high heels clicking with each step. "I'm not Miss Party Planner Extraordinaire, but I know who to call." Austin saw her nose flare as she hugged her future sister in law, no doubt scenting the subtle change he'd detected earlier. "Go have fun with Kenz, spend some of Austin's money. You need new clothes for… school as well."

Charlotte's cheeks flushed with the prettiest red blush he'd ever seen, and his highly developed senses felt the tidal wave of heat from three feet away.

After Kensington swept Charlotte from the room, Austin turned to Israel. "I don't know how you arranged it—

but thank you." Israel grinned like a kid caught with his hand in the cookie jar.

"I was on the phone with him when I heard your conversation in the control room." Israel must have noted Austin's frown because he laughed and shook his head. "I'd already run the staff out, big brother. It was a given there was going to be a thrown down when your mate realized you hadn't been kidding about her losing her position as your Administrative Assistant. I reprogrammed the monitoring equipment in your office. Everything will record as usual until the system recognizes Charlotte's voice. As soon as she speaks? Blackout for the security team. Once she's gone, your new assistant will notify the control room, and they'll reset everything.

"Face it, big brother, you're probably a bigger target now because you're going to be married to one of the most sought after and well-connected magicals in the world. Anyone who is around the two of you for more than thirty seconds will know the way to influence one of you is to get to the other." Asia had merely stated the obvious, but her message wasn't lost on him.

As one of the youngest billionaires in the world, Austin had been forced to become more security aware over the past couple of years. Kidnapping and ransom demands were a constant risk. The danger would be exponential now. Shaking his head, Austin redirected his thoughts to planning a wedding. He sent off a quick message to Kensington, letting him know they were to buy a dress today. Austin wasn't waiting weeks for a dress to be ordered from some damned boutique on the other side of the globe.

The three of them brainstormed and in ten minutes, divided the duties into manageable lists. By noon, he, Asia, and Israel had made all the calls and successfully planned what Austin hoped would be Charlotte's dream wedding. Neither London nor Brooklyn would be able to attend, but he'd promised to live-stream the entire evening affair for them.

"Why does it take women a year to plan a wedding? Hell, we planned this one in less than three hours." Of course, they hadn't needed to book a venue months in advance, and they'd called in enough favors to get a florist and caterer to work them into their already tight schedules. When they hadn't been able to get the photographer, Asia insisted was the best, to take his call, he'd called Tobi West who promptly called her mother-in-law.

In ten minutes, Lilly West called, assuring them the flamboyant photographer had not only been thrilled to take the job, he'd be doing so at a reduced rate. It turned out the man had been angling for a guest invitation to Prairie Winds for several years, and Lilly had promised to make sure he had his invitation before Austin and Charlotte's wedding. Great, now I owe Kent and Kyle West a favor, along with everyone else in his phone's extensive contact list.

"Bet your ungrateful ass is much happier now about all the upgrades I insisted on for our mutual outdoor living space. Remember all the whining you did about delays and overages?" Asia was leaning back against his desk, long legs crossed at the ankle, blowing on her lacquered nails, pretending to buff them on her jacket lapel. "Yes, indeed. The perfect location for your nuptials was right outside your door. What was it you called me? Oh yes, now I remember. You said I was a combination of Joss and Main, Home Depot, and Lizzie Borden." Asia's mocking tone and cutting words made Israel spew water all over the tablet he'd been working on.

"Fuck, Asia. Give a guy some warning next time. Austin, you didn't really compare your sister to Lizzie Borden, did you? What the ever-loving hell?"

Casting Asia a withering look he knew was a wasted effort, Austin shook his head in defeat. "Somebody order us some damned lunch, I'm starving. And find an interior designer. I want to get started on a nursery while we're on our honeymoon."

Israel and Asia both stared at him, their mouths gaping open in surprise. Perfect. As usual, the only way to shut up his siblings was to shock them to their toes.

Chapter Twenty

One week later

CHARLOTTE STARED AT herself in the full-length mirror in the bedroom she shared with Austin. "Who are you?" The woman gazing back at her was glamorous—hair perfectly styled, makeup professionally applied, dressed in the most beautiful wedding gown she'd ever seen. Warm hands caressed her bare shoulders, causing her to look up, meeting her mate's heated gaze.

"She's the most beautiful woman in the world—and she belongs to me."

He was becoming more protective by the day, and she was starting to worry at some point, she might find herself locked in a mountain cabin with twelve-foot-high, electrified, razor wire fence and a moat surrounding what he would no doubt call a retreat. His smile and a snort of laughter behind them brought her attention back to the heat racing from where his fingers kneaded the tight muscles along the top of her shoulders down her torso all the way to her sex.

"Damn, you amaze me, Charlotte. Your mind works at Mach speed, but jumping from razor wire to a needy pussy is a leap even for you."

Israel's teasing tone broke the tension, and despite how nervous she'd been all day, Charlotte let laughter bubble up from the depths of her soul. Looking into Austin's eyes, she felt the nervousness of the past few days drain away.

"I'm going to love having brothers and sisters, but most of all, I'm going to love being your wife, mate, submissive, and the mother of your children." Seeing her Alpha mate's eyes go glassy with unshed tears made her wonder if her already full heart would burst.

"Could you two wrap this up before I get a cavity?" Israel's sarcasm didn't fool her. His heart longed to find his own mate despite his insistence otherwise. "Big brother, you need to get outside before Asia blows in here like a Cat Five hurricane—you know how she is about schedules." When Austin glared at his younger brother, Israel shrugged. "I just figured you wanted all your parts functional on your honeymoon... but whatever."

Charlotte couldn't hold back her laughter. Knowing Austin had put an indefinite hold on development in Cedar Bayou filled her with a sense of relief she hadn't expected.

Lifting her hand and placing it over his heart, Austin stared down into her eyes as he snapped something around her wrist. Looking down, Charlotte was surprised to see a glittering platinum bracelet. *A charm bracelet?*

"I'll add charms as we grow together, Charlotte."

Looking down, she felt her eyes fill with tears when she saw a pair of baby booties and a charm-shaped ring, complete with a sparkling diamond. There was a book charm that made her smile. The small heart with a hand cut from the center—the international symbol for charity—

was a nod to her new assignment developing the Adler Charitable Foundation. But it was the mixed metal wolf that brought her to tears. She hadn't been able to shift since the night on the beach, but he'd acknowledged her magic manifesting itself that night when nothing had mattered but protecting her mate.

"It's beautiful. I'll cherish it always." Her words were nearly covered by the sound of the door banging open as Asia Adler stormed into the room.

"Chop chop, people. Let's get this show on the road. Good grief, it's taken longer to get the bride dressed and down the aisle than it did to plan the whole wedding." Israel, Austin, and Charlotte all burst out laughing as Asia hustle Austin from the room.

"Are you ready, sweetheart?" Israel pulled her into a tight hug before stepping back to hold out his arm for her. He was going to walk her down the aisle in her dad's absence. Making their way down the hall, Charlotte felt the familiar tingling dancing over the surface of her skin, making the hair on the back of her neck stand on end. Smiling, she turned to Israel, pulling him to a stop. Before she could explain, her dad appeared in a swirl of gray smoke.

"You didn't think I was going to let someone else walk my only daughter down the aisle, did you?" Charlotte bit her lip to keep from bursting into tears. Damn, it seemed like she was becoming more emotional every day. "Your mother and aunt can handle things for a couple of hours." Charlotte learned years ago to not take the bait. Her dad often complained his wife and sister-in-law put work ahead of everything else in their lives, but he rarely acted against them. For the first time in her life, Charlotte felt like her dad had made her a priority.

She took her dad's arm and moved in front of the door that would lead her into the outdoor living area and her dream wedding. No one had allowed her anywhere near the rooftop patio since decorating began the day before, insisting they wanted it to be a surprise. As the curtain was drawn back, Charlotte felt Austin's calm presence even before she could see him.

You'll always be my first priority, Charlotte. Your safety and happiness are the first things I think about when I wake up and the last thought I have as I fall to sleep.

"He sent a message to me, you know?" Turning to look at her dad, Charlotte wondered what he was talking about. "I don't even want to think about the strings he had to pull to get it passed along, but he made it very clear how important it was for me to be here." Pressing a gentle kiss against her forehead, he gave her a smile filled with something that looked too much like guilt. "He's a good man, Charley. I'd have whisked you out of here otherwise."

He could have tried. Now, let's do this before Asia has a stroke. Come to me, Charlotte.

Epilogue

PARIS ADLER KEPT her strokes even, despite the stalker standing like a damned sentry at one end. Why did he choose tonight to show up? Crap on a cactus, wouldn't you know the one night she decided to go skinny dipping, Sheriff Snoop decides to show up? Who the hell drops in after nine o'clock at night? Hell, even her college friends had better manners. Trinity Stone could just stand there for all she cared. If he didn't have the courtesy to call, she didn't feel any need to play hostess. Damn it. The simple truth was, Trinity Stone unnerved her on so many levels, she ended up feeling like an inept teenager when he was around.

Missing Austin and Charlotte's wedding was going to break her heart, but she'd promised to house-sit, and her sister was still enjoying her honeymoon. Paris was starting to suspect London's husbands were going to continue extending their stay until they talked her workaholic sister into taking time off, and she felt up to traveling. London had done a good job of putting on a brave face with the other siblings, but Paris had surprised her one morning and knew how sick she'd been.

Her new brothers-in-law had fed her a lame bullshit

line about worrying about the house which was absurd since it was inside a secured perimeter fence. She'd barely managed to keep from rolling her eyes, but in the end, she hadn't put up much of a fight. She'd finished all her school work and had already gotten her diploma.

Austin was going to be pissed when he found out she'd opted out of participating in graduation, but as their granny had always said… he had the same clothes to get glad in. Paris knew she should have told her family about the trouble she'd been having, but in the beginning, the situation had seemed so manageable, she hadn't wanted them to think she couldn't handle things herself. When the problem continued to escalate, she'd hesitated because she'd dreaded the lecture she'd been certain was coming.

Flipping over and pushing off the pool's smooth wall, Paris let her eyes flicker over the man watching her with such focused intensity, she wondered if he was reading her mind. *Don't be ridiculous, if he could read your mind, he'd know about California, and that you think he's the hottest asswipe on the planet.*

TRINITY WAS STILL fuming about the phone call he'd received this morning. He'd met Luke Grayson several months ago when Paris's older sister, Brooklyn, was a patient at Evan Monroe's clinic. Luke and Brooklyn were now engaged and living in his secluded New Mexico mountain home. The remote location didn't keep him from being one of the best computer consultants in the world—what Luke called research, the rest of the world called hacking, but Uncle Sam was smart enough to utilize his skills rather than smother them.

One of their last nights at the resort in the Caribbean, the minx swimming laps in her damned birthday suit had defied him, putting herself in danger when he'd specifically told her to stay where he'd put her. He'd paddled her, and she'd fucking come. He'd been shocked, and she'd been mortified. Fucking hell, he'd never had a sub come on the fourth swat, and he'd damned well never had one so embarrassed by an orgasm, she'd run from the room. She'd talked someone into whisking her off to the airport, and the brat had been one step ahead of him all the way home.

Trinity managed to stay away for a week, hoping it would give him time to reassess the situation with a cooler head. He'd known she had a job interview this morning to teach at the private school his pack was starting the next school year. She didn't know it yet, but this afternoon, the board had voted unanimously to hire her. London's fathers-in-law, Jameson and Jack Monroe, had bowed out of the interview due to a conflict of interest, but once the board hired Paris, they'd lobbied for a compensation package she wouldn't be able to turn down.

Smiling to himself, Trinity knew the Monroe's well, and their motives weren't entirely altruistic. Pack children weren't always safe in public schools, so the decision was made to build a private school on land inside the enormous secured area owned by the packs who'd joined forces generations ago.

Keeping their pregnant daughter-in-law happy was the Monroe patriarchs real priority, and they were wise enough to know having her youngest sister nearby would be a huge help to London in more ways than most people knew. From what Trinity heard from his Aunt Julia, mother to the former and current pack leaders, the brilliant researcher was struggling with morning sickness severe enough, her mates were postponing their return home until things settled a bit for her.

He shook his head to bring his thoughts back to the hellion pounding the water in front of him. As a shifter, his senses were keener than most people's, and when it came to Paris Adler, it seemed like every molecule in his body was tuned to her frequency. He could feel not only her frustration with his sudden appearance but her rapidly growing fatigue as well. The little hellcat was going to drown if she didn't stop soon.

Moving to the shadowed side of the pool, he chuckled when her uncertainty rolled through his mind. He wasn't sure what her magicals gifts were and sent up a silent prayer to the Great Goddess she hadn't imbued Paris with the ability to zap him with lightning. As she neared, he stepped forward, grabbing her upper arm before she could turn. At six foot seven, Trinity had plenty of strength and leverage to pull the slender, five foot three brat from the water.

"What the fuck?" Naked, dripping wet, and spitting mad, she swiped long blond hair from her eyes with her free hand and glared up at him. "You can't just yank me out of the water like an errant child." He didn't bother disagreeing because it was obvious he absolutely could.

"We need to have a chat, Paris." He saw her eyes widen in surprise at his use of her name.

"You could have just called."

And have her ignore his calls? No, he'd known better

than to give her the chance to keep him at arm's length. She might not have told her family about the situation in California, but she was damned well going to talk to him. When he started to pull her toward the cabinet where he knew the towels were stored, she pulled back, trying to balk.

Shaking his head at her stubborn attitude, he asked, "Are you sure this is the way you want this to go? Hell, I'd like nothing better than to keep you stark naked while we talk because believe me, the view is spectacular." He let his eyes move over her in a sensual slide. "Baby, the moonlight loves you. It highlights your tightly peaked nipples, drawing my eyes to the beads of water racing to the sweet tips. Hell, watching those drops let go of your pink nipples might just become my new favorite pastime."

She firmed her mouth into a straight line but had the wisdom to keep her sass under wraps. Wrapping herself in a plush towel he handed her from the warming cabinet, Paris spun around so quickly, water droplets flew from the ends of her long, blonde locks. He saw her lips part to speak but beat her to the punch.

"Tell me about David Lamb, Paris." He felt a wave of emotion wash over him, the mixture of fear and disbelief so strong, he knew she was fighting the urge to run. "Talk to me, sweetheart." He'd learned to expect anything from the youngest Adler—what he hadn't anticipated was her launching herself into his arms.

The End

Books by Avery Gale

The Adlers
Brooklyn
London
Austin

The ShadowDance Club
Katarina's Return – Book One
Jenna's Submission – Book Two
Rissa's Recovery – Book Three
Trace & Tori – Book Four
Reborn as Bree – Book Five
Red Clouds Dancing – Book Six
Perfect Picture – Book Seven

Club Isola
Capturing Callie – Book One
Healing Holly – Book Two
Claiming Abby – Book Three

Masters of the Prairie Winds Club
Out of the Storm
Saving Grace
Jen's Journey
Bound Treasure
Punishing for Pleasure
Accidental Trifecta
Missionary Position
Another Second Chance
Star-Crossed Miracles
Dusted Star
Lilly's Choice

The Wolf Pack Series
Mated – Book One
Fated Magic – Book Two
Tempted by Darkness – Book Three

The Knights of the Boardroom
Book One
Book Two
Book Three

The Morgan Brothers of Montana
Coral Hearts – Book One
Dancing with Deception – Book Two
Caged Songbird – Book Three
Game On – Book Four
Well Bred – Book Five

Mountain Mastery
Well Written
Savannah's Sentinel
Sheltering Reagan

The Christmas Painting
Taking Out the Mother of the Bride

I would love to hear from you!

Email:
avery.gale@ymail.com

Website:
www.averygale.com

Facebook:
facebook.com/avery.gale.3

Twitter:
@avery_gale